“What do yo
wedding? Tomorrow.”

“All right,” Dana said.

Her head spun. How had this happened? Forty-eight hours ago she’d spilled coffee on him and vowed to find a way to clear the Hewitt name. Now she was marrying the guy and *changing* her name to McCormack. In the contrition department, that seemed excessive. She reminded herself that it was to their mutual advantage.

She almost believed that. This deal was mostly for her, but she was desperate. Somehow she would make it up to him. But she was going into *this* marriage with her eyes wide open. Her terms. She was in control. Yesiree.

But when Quentin turned the full power of his blue eyes on her, she couldn’t help thinking that control was such a tenuous thing….

* * * * *

Don’t miss any of the four titles in the STORKVILLE, USA series—

THOSE MATCHMAKING BABIES
by Marie Ferrarella (8/00, SR#1462)

HIS EXPECTANT NEIGHBOR
by Susan Meier (9/00, SR#1468)

THE ACQUIRED BRIDE
by Teresa Southwick (10/00, SR#1474)

HER HONOR-BOUND LAWMAN
by Karen Rose Smith (11/00 SR #1480)

Dear Reader,

As Silhouette's yearlong anniversary celebration continues, Romance again delivers six unique stories about the poignant journey from courtship to commitment.

Teresa Southwick invites you back to STORKVILLE, USA, where a wealthy playboy has the gossips stumped with his latest transaction: *The Acquired Bride*...and her triplet kids! *New York Times* bestselling author Kasey Michaels contributes the second title in THE CHANDLERS REQUEST... miniseries, *Jessie's Expecting.* Judy Christenberry spins off her popular THE CIRCLE K SISTERS with a story involving a blizzard, a roadside motel with one bed left, a gorgeous, honor-bound rancher...and his *Snowbound Sweetheart.*

New from Donna Clayton is SINGLE DOCTOR DADS! In the premiere story of this wonderful series, a first-time father strikes *The Nanny Proposal* with a woman whose timely hiring quickly proves less serendipitous and more carefully, *lovingly,* staged.... Lilian Darcy pens yet another edgy, uplifting story with *Raising Baby Jane.* And debut author Jackie Braun delivers pure romantic fantasy as a down-on-her-luck waitress receives an intriguing order from the man of her dreams: *One Fiancée To Go, Please.*

Next month, look for the exciting finales of STORKVILLE, USA and THE CHANDLERS REQUEST... And the wait is over as Carolyn Zane's BRUBAKER BRIDES make their grand reappearance!

Happy Reading!

Mary-Theresa Hussey

Mary-Theresa Hussey
Senior Editor

Please address questions and book requests to:
Silhouette Reader Service
U.S.: 3010 Walden Ave., P.O. Box 1325, Buffalo, NY 14269
Canadian: P.O. Box 609, Fort Erie, Ont. L2A 5X3

The Acquired Bride

TERESA SOUTHWICK

Published by Silhouette Books
America's Publisher of Contemporary Romance

Special thanks and acknowledgment are given to Teresa Southwick for her contribution to the Storkville, USA series.

SILHOUETTE BOOKS

ISBN 0-373-19474-9

THE ACQUIRED BRIDE

This edition published by arrangement with Harlequin Books S.A.

Visit Silhouette at www.eHarlequin.com

Printed in U.S.A.

Books by Teresa Southwick

Silhouette Romance

Wedding Rings and Baby Things #1209
The Bachelor's Baby #1233
**A Vow, a Ring, a Baby Swing* #1349
The Way to a Cowboy's Heart #1383
**And Then He Kissed Me* #1405
**With a Little T.L.C.* #1421
The Acquired Bride #1474

Silhouette Books

The Fortunes of Texas
Shotgun Vows

*The Marchetti Family

TERESA SOUTHWICK

is a native Californian who has recently moved to Texas. Living with her husband of twenty-five years and two handsome sons, she is surrounded by heroes. Reading has been her passion since she was a girl. She couldn't be more delighted that her dream of writing full-time has come true. Her favorite things include: holding a baby, the fragrance of jasmine, walks on the beach, the patter of rain on the roof and, above all, happy endings.

Teresa also writes historical romance novels under the same name.

Storkville folks hardly remember the day the town bore another name—because the residents keep bearing bundles of joy! No longer known for its safe neighborhoods and idyllic landscape, Storkville is baby-bootie capital of the world! We even have a legend for the explosion of "uplets"—"When the stork visits, he bestows many bouncing bundles on those whose love is boundless!" Of course, some—Gertie Anderson—still insist a certain lemonade recipe, which is "guaranteed" to help along prospective mothers, is the real stork! But whether the little darlings come from the cabbage patch or the delivery room, Storkville folks never underestimate the beauty of holding a child—or the enchantment of first love and the wonder of second chance....

Chapter One

He'd been slimed!

Quentin McCormack looked down and watched cotton candy, Hawaiian punch and chocolate mix together and slide down his leg. The triple whammy.

Then he met the worried, gray-eyed gaze of the pint-sized linebacker who'd collided with him. Contrition was written all over his face and Quentin hadn't the heart to reprimand the little guy, even though the trousers were new and expensive. He also hadn't a clue how old the boy was, but he was definitely too little to be wandering around alone.

"You okay, buddy?" he asked.

The boy, who barely came up to Quentin's knee, nodded tentatively.

"Where's your mom and dad?"

His only response was a shrug. Quentin surveyed the lunchtime crowd. It was August and hot. Hannah Caldwell had just cut the ribbon to open her new day-care center. Most everyone in town was there for the ceremony because Storkville took its responsibility to children very seriously. Which made him wonder who would let their child wander unattended.

He glanced at shop windows up and down Main Street. "Do your parents work nearby?" he asked.

"Mommy works at bad nets and boots," he said proudly.

Quentin frowned. Sounded like a sporting-goods store named by someone unclear on the concept. He must be missing something.

Just then he heard a female, panic-tinged voice calling, "Lukas!" He looked down at the child. "What's your name?"

"Wookie," he answered.

"Like the Star Wars character?" he asked. He wouldn't be surprised. For all he knew the boy was speaking an alien language. Ditto, he thought when the child looked at him as if he had two heads.

The crowd parted and two feet from him, Quentin saw a frantic-looking woman holding the hands of two little girls with tear-streaked faces. His breath caught as he stared at her. Shoulder-length, chestnut brown curls framed a heart-shaped face with the biggest, most expressive gray eyes he'd ever seen. She wasn't tall, maybe five foot two, but her slender body, with curves in all the right places, was his fantasy come to life.

Lightning.

A direct hit. He couldn't have felt more zapped if he'd been standing in an electrical storm holding a kite string with a key attached.

Because of the crowd on blocked-off Main Street, she didn't notice him or his new little friend. They were standing in front of the sprawling three-story Victorian house with wraparound porch and enclosed backyard containing play equipment that was now BabyCare. To get the woman's attention, he held up his hand, then curled his fingers into his palm when he noticed it was shaking. She finally looked directly at him and he pointed down.

"Is he by any chance yours?"

Bingo, he thought when her shoulders drooped with relief. She was beside him in three strides and squatted down on a level with the child.

"Lukie, you scared me half to death," she said in a voice that was three parts concern and one part anger. Then she pulled him into her arms for a viselike hug. "Don't *ever* run off like that again, young man."

"His name isn't Wookie?" Quentin asked.

She stood and smiled, taking his breath away for the second time in two minutes. "His name is Lukas and articulating L's is a challenge for a three-year-old."

"Hewwo, Mommy," the child said, his red-stained mouth turning up in a grin.

"Hi, Lukie." She looked back at Quentin and shrugged. "See what I mean? His sisters have the same problem."

"They're *all* three?" he asked, surveying the children, who were about the same size. Stunned, he watched her nod. "You must be from Storkville," he said, shaking his head.

"You mean because the stork who visits Storkville bestows many bouncing bundles on those whose love is boundless?" she asked, her gray eyes twinkling.

"That's the legend," he concurred.

"I think the stork had a navigational malfunction that day because he visited me in Omaha. And—" she glanced at the three children with infinite love "—I don't know if he bestowed bouncing bundles as much as the triple whammy."

"My exact thought," he said, remembering his close encounter of the gooey kind. "But not about children. Cotton candy, red punch and chocolate is an awful lot of junk food for a little guy like this," Quentin commented. "Not to mention the fact that he's running around unsupervised, Mrs.—"

Her eyes suddenly reminded him of a sky on a stormy day and he braced himself for a zap of *bad* lightning.

"Dana Hewitt," she said introducing herself. "I'm aware that a three-year-old needs supervision, Mr.—"

"McCormack. Quentin McCormack."

If possible, she looked even more annoyed. "Of *the* McCormacks, Storkville's founding family?"

"The very same." So she knew who he was and that he didn't have to wonder where his next dollar was coming from.

"Great," she muttered. Then her chin lifted slightly, reinforcing her defensive body language. "Do you have children, Mr. McCormack?"

"I'm not married," he said.

"That's not what I asked. Your marital status doesn't preclude fathering children."

"For me it does. I would never be that irresponsible." He met her gaze and realized that she barely came up to his chin. He was six feet tall, which made her—really small.

"Have you ever heard the saying 'Never judge a man—or woman, until you've walked in their shoes'?"

"Yes."

"Good. Here's another one. When you have triplets, we'll talk." She reclaimed the hands of her two still-sniffling girls. "Not that it's any of your business, but each of the children was allowed to choose one treat. While I was paying for them, Lukie grabbed his and the girls' too and took off while my back was turned."

"I see." What he didn't see was where her husband fit into all this. Why wasn't he with her to help corral three small children? "I didn't mean to judge. You're right. I haven't a clue how to deal with one child, let alone three the same age. Sorry."

"Apology accepted," she said. When she looked at her son, her anger faded and a different sort of look suffused her features, an expression that was both mad and tender. "You are in a lot of trouble, young man. Never, ever run off like that," she said again.

"Wanted a b'loon," the child said, his bottom lip slightly thrust out. "No time out, Mommy." He shook his head and backed up into Quentin's leg.

"I know you wanted a balloon. But we can't always have everything we want when we want it. Especially on our budget."

One of the little girls looked tearfully up at Dana. "Mommy, make Wookie give me my cotton candy."

"Me, too," the other girl chimed in.

"Taking your sisters' treats..." Dana heaved an exasperated sigh and shook her head at her son. "Your attention span isn't long enough for the time out you deserve. Give Molly back her cotton candy and Kelly her chocolate." She looked closer and for the first time seemed to notice his empty hands. "You couldn't have eaten all of that so fast. The spirit is more than willing, but the tummy is way too small."

Quentin saw the exact moment when she started to put together what happened. Her gaze went to her son's sticky empty hands, then to the circle of goo surrounding his own Italian leather loafers, then finally up to his designer pant legs that were now so stiff they could stand up by themselves.

Her eyes and mouth opened wide and rounded into Os. ''Good heavens,'' she said. ''Please tell me, *my* son didn't do that to you.''

''Don't worry about it. Accidents happen.''

''Oh, Lukie, tell Mr. McCormack sorry.''

The boy looked up at him. ''Sorry, Mr. Mac.''

''It's okay, pal,'' he said, ruffling the boy's hair.

''It's Mr. McCormack,'' she corrected her son.

''That's a pretty big mouthful,'' he said. ''Mac's fine.''

''I can't tell you how sorry I am about this Mr. Mc—''

''Please call me Quentin.''

''All right, Quentin,'' she said. ''I insist you let me have your trousers cleaned for you.''

''That's a tough one. Unless you want me to drop 'em right here in front of God and everyone on Main Street.''

She blushed and the look went straight to his heart, infiltrating his defenses without firing a shot. Of course it didn't hurt that she had a sweet smile, with full, sensuous lips, and curls around her face that looked as if a man had run his hands through her hair while kissing her senseless. The combination was his second triple whammy in the last five minutes.

She shook her head. ''No, I'd appreciate it if you didn't drop your pants right here. I want to do the right thing, but something tells me a public display of that nature would be stickier than the puddle at your feet.''

''I agree,'' he said grinning. He had a feeling his smile was way too wide, but maybe it would hide his reaction to her.

''But I insist you send me the cleaning bill.''

"That's not necessary."

"But how can I repay you for this?" she asked.

"You can answer a question for me."

"All right," she agreed.

"What kind of establishment is Bad Nets and Boots?"

"Excuse me?" She looked at him blankly.

"Lukas told me that's where you work."

She laughed, a merry sound that knocked on the door closing off his heart. Avoiding emotional entanglements was his stock in trade. He'd learned that women were more interested in his checkbook balance than in the man who signed the checks.

"I manage a store here in town. It's called Bassinets and Booties," she explained.

"Ah. That explains why I've never seen you before."

"You mean you've never shopped our aisles of smiles containing diapers, cribs and layettes?"

"Can't say I have." He couldn't help joining in her laughter. Then, he asked, "And where does Mr. Hewitt work?"

He wanted to kick himself when a dark look erased the merriment from her face. In its place she wore a pinched expression that pulled her full lips into a straight line. "There is no Mr. Hewitt. He passed away."

"I'm sorry," he said automatically.

Except he found himself very much *not* sorry that she was unattached. But he couldn't help wondering if part of the Storkville legend had touched her long-distance. Was her love for the husband she'd lost boundless? He hoped not.

As soon as he'd thought it, he was appalled. What had gotten into him? He'd been slimed on the outside and now he knew it was merely a visible manifestation of what he was like on the inside. Worse, he didn't know what to say to get past the awkward moment.

He could only come up with, "You're very lucky to have the children."

"Don't I know it. And no one is going to take them from me," she added emphatically.

"Why would anyone take them?" he asked, puzzled.

"A better question would be why would anyone but me want them," she shot back. "They're demanding, rambunctious, active. They do everything in triplicate." She nodded forcefully. "But Molly, Kelly and Lukas are my whole life."

"I envy you. My whole life is business and it's not nearly as exciting as your children."

"Should I be flattered or insulted? What kind of business are you in?" she asked.

Her face appeared innocence itself, but he read between the lines of her question to another one: *How much money do you make?*

"I deal in investments. Finances. A little of this and that," he said vaguely. "That's not the same as the commitment you've made. Your children are lucky to be on the receiving end of such unconditional love."

"They might trade a small percentage for an extra pair of hands," she said ruefully. "Sometimes these three seem like twenty. But thank goodness I found a job in Storkville. I relocated here about six months ago and found that it's a wonderful place to raise children. If Lukie had gotten away from me anywhere else—" She suppressed a shudder at the unthinkable.

"Why did you leave Omaha?"

There was a troubled, faraway expression on her face. But all she said was, "I had no family left. I'm an only child and my parents are both gone. And—the memories there were too much. I decided to start over here with the children."

"It's Storkville's gain," he said.

"Thank you." She glanced guiltily at his pants. "Not necessarily yours, though. Are you certain you won't let me pick up the cost of dry cleaning?"

Clear, beautiful gray eyes looked into his own. Odd, he thought. He wanted to drown in her eyes. He blinked a couple of times, mentally shaking himself. He was a by-the-numbers businessman, not a poet. What was he thinking—*drown in a woman's eyes?* Get a grip, McCormack.

He might have been able to rein in his acute response if the rest of her hadn't inspired him, too. Her petite form fit nicely into a pair of black slacks topped by a black-trimmed beige sweater. Her breasts, not too big or too small, filled out the sweater perfectly, as if it was made for her. In fact, he couldn't help thinking that she would fit him nicely, as if she was made for him too. Whoa, Mac.

"Mommy, I hafta go." One of the little girls—Kelly or Molly?—tugged on her hand.

No, don't go, he thought. He felt like he could stand there and talk to her forever.

Dana looked down at her daughter. "Okay, sweetie."

Dana turned back to Quentin and said, "I think I'd better get the children home. Let me know if you change your mind about the cleaning charges," she offered.

"I won't. But thanks."

Dana released one of the girls and instructed Molly and Kelly to hold hands tight. Then she took her son's sticky fingers in a firm grip. "I appreciate your understanding about Lukie. Somehow, I'll figure out a way to thank you. Goodbye, Quentin."

He searched for something to say that would keep her there a little longer, but came up empty.

He watched her walk away, and the crowd swallowed Dana Hewitt and her brood before his lightning-fried brain functioned normally again. He realized he hadn't asked for her phone number. He could always drop by the store, or…

No.

This was for the best. He would bet everything he owned that she was still getting over the loss of her husband. But because of all he owned, it was necessary to question the motives of every woman he met. And Dana was especially risky. He was pretty sure she didn't have a lot of money to spare.

He looked down at his pants. In spite of the spectacle he must make, he grinned. Cute kids—especially Lukas. But the fruit didn't fall far from the tree. Cute mom.

Now he would do himself a favor and forget her.

"I guess that does it." Cleland Knox, owner of Storkville's insurance agency and president of the chamber of commerce, consulted his notes.

It was October first and the merchants of Storkville were meeting in the town hall to discuss the tentative schedule of holiday events, from Halloween to Christmas and New Year's. When finalized, it would be printed and posted all over town.

Dana, sitting in for her boss, fidgeted in her chair. She wondered if her hair and clothes looked all right. Normally, she didn't question her appearance. Ordinarily, she did the best she could with what she had. But tonight wasn't normal or ordinary. Quentin McCormack was sitting behind her.

Goose bumps that had nothing to do with the chill in

the hall skittered up and down her arms. She had carried around a mental picture of the brown-haired, blue-eyed hunk ever since she'd first laid eyes on him in August. His cover-model good looks had been responsible for her not noticing right away what Lukie had done to him. And that was because her gaze had only strayed as far from his face as to his impossibly broad shoulders and his flat abdomen. Only later had she noticed his muscular thighs encased in the expensive material—and covered with gunk.

"Is there any other business?" The C.O.C. president interrupted her delicious yet mortifying daydream.

Dana raised her hand. "Mr. Knox?"

He looked into the crowd. "The chair recognizes Mrs. Hewitt of Bassinets and Booties."

She suppressed a grin at his formality. He and his wife Grace were regulars in the store, frequently buying toys, clothes and furniture for their four grandchildren.

"Mr. President, I just wanted to make sure that the Bassinets and Booties holiday party, fashion show and raffle are on the schedule. I didn't see it on the rough draft."

Dana had just come up with the idea a couple days ago. Her boss had loved her suggestion for the store's Christmas promotion this year. Every merchant planned something and the events were staggered so that people could get to them all. It was also a last big push that boosted sales through Christmas and the end of the year.

Cleland scanned the paper in his hand and nodded. "I have it penciled in here. Don't worry. It will be on the final schedule. Second Saturday in December," he confirmed.

"That's right," she agreed. "Thank you."

"The weekend after that is Santa's visit to the kids at BabyCare. That okay with you, Hannah?"

"Wonderful," the woman sitting to Dana's left answered. "And don't forget the costume party for the kids at the day-care center the week before Halloween."

The blond highlights in Hannah's brown hair glowed beneath the town hall's fluorescent lights. But that was nothing compared to the sparkle in her brown eyes. And that had everything to do with Jackson Caldwell, the love of her life, who was sitting beside her. Her face was so bright, she could have lit the town of Storkville for the entire holiday season, Halloween and Thanksgiving included.

Dana sighed. She envied them. They'd been childhood sweethearts who had recently been reunited and rekindled their love. Together they were caring for, and falling in love with, the twins abandoned at the day-care center a few days after she'd first met Quentin.

What would it be like, she wondered, to find a love that neither time nor adversity could kill? Her one and only experience with romance hadn't shown her. And she wasn't likely to get another chance—even if she wanted one. Her job hindered her from meeting unattached men. And then there was the issue of her three children. They would be enough to scare even the most intrepid man into a monastery. But she adored them and they came first.

"Mr. President?"

Dana would have known Quentin's deep voice anywhere. She blushed, remembering how its timbre lowered a notch as he joked about dropping his pants right there on Main Street so that she could have them cleaned. Her heart beat faster at the image. He was pretty spectacular with his pants *on* and she suspected he was something of a religious experience with them off. Merely an objective observation. Her heart might be romantically challenged, but her eyesight was twenty-twenty, uncorrected.

"The floor recognizes Quentin McCormack."

"I just want to remind everyone of the Halloween costume party at the McCormack estate on Saturday, October twenty-eighth. Invitations will go out in the next couple of days. But my parents and I would like you to put the date on the calendar. We're hoping for a big turnout."

"Got it down, Quentin. Anyone else?" Cleland scanned the room. Satisfied that no one else had anything to add, he banged his gavel. "Meeting adjourned. My mouth has been watering for some of Doris and Vern Feeney's cherry pie. They were kind enough to bring some over from the diner."

"I've brought some of my special lemonade," Aunt Gertie piped up. In her late sixties, she was a petite, silver-haired woman with twinkling brown eyes and a magic brew "guaranteed" to help along prospective mothers trying to get pregnant.

A line formed beside the refreshment table. Dana didn't even need to look to know who had stepped behind her. Quentin McCormack. The scent of his cologne was permanently embedded in her memory. He was close enough so that she could feel the heat of his body. And what a very tall body he had, she thought, her heart fluttering. Okay, so being romantically challenged didn't preclude some involuntary spasms.

Dana poured herself coffee, then glanced at him. "Hello."

Her knees went weak at his oh-so-attractive smile. She debated the pros and cons of turning completely around.

On the one hand, not looking at him would be incredibly rude. On the other, if she faced him, she would have to deal with the full effects of Storkville's sexiest man.

She took a deep breath and turned around.

"Hi," he answered. "I see you're avoiding Aunt Gertie's lemonade," he said, ladling some into his cup. "It's made with Storkville springwater," he added.

"So I've heard, along with the rumor about it causing pregnancy. But I see you're not afraid."

Grinning, he said, "For obvious reasons. But you shouldn't be either. The last time I took biology, they were teaching that there's only one time-honored way to produce a baby," he said, his voice lowering with the suggestive comment. "And it doesn't include storks or finding bundles under cabbage leaves."

"I'm not taking any chances," she said firmly.

"For three very good reasons." He chuckled.

As she spooned sugar into her cup, she concentrated on controlling her shaking hands. He was a tycoon—Storkville's answer to Donald Trump—according to teenage town gossip Penny Sue Lipton, who worked after school at the day-care center. Still, the man had been more than kind to her son, even after being on the business end of his cotton candy. Nine out of ten tycoons would have chewed Lukie up and spit him out, not asked him to call them Mr. Mac. However much she rationalized her reaction to him, she would be lying to herself if she didn't admit that she found Quentin McCormack super-appealing.

With her coffee carefully cradled in both hands, she tried to inch away from the table, but she was trapped. People were behind her and one incredibly sexy tycoon blocked her from the front. She blew on the contents of her cup as she searched for an escape route, or failing that, something to say. "How are you?" she finally asked.

"Fine. And you?"

"Busy," she answered automatically.

He studied her face. "You look tired."

"Just distracted," she said.

"If anyone else said that to me, I'd figure it was just small talk. In your case, you've got reasons times three why your focus is fragmented. How are the kids?"

"Great," she said.

"Are they excited about the holidays coming?"

"That's hard to say. They remember a little from last year. But it wasn't a very happy time." The expression on his handsome face was so kind and sympathetic she found herself telling him more. "Their father was in an automobile accident almost a year ago."

"I'm sorry," he said automatically.

"He was in a coma for a week before he died on Christmas Eve. It was a rough time for them. Their recollections are vague, thank goodness. I hope to replace those memories with happy ones this year." But if her in-laws had their way, that wasn't likely. She couldn't suppress the shiver of apprehension that slithered through her.

"Is something wrong, Dana?" he asked.

"Nothing I can't handle," she answered.

Just then Cleland Knox, in line behind Dana, backed into her, knocking her forward. The sudden movement caused her to launch the contents of her cup. It arced onto the front of Quentin's sport coat, the stark white shirt beneath, and the front of his pants.

Stunned, she stared open-mouthed at the liquid soaking into his shirt and dripping down his flat-as-a-washboard abdomen. "Oh, Quentin, I'm so sorry."

Quickly, she grabbed the stack of napkins from the table beside her and began to blot him. At least the coffee had cooled and didn't scald him. If only she could say the same for herself—she was hot and bothered. She tried to ignore her response to touching the abdomen she'd admired. But her stomach fluttered like a thousand butterflies in flight.

"I can't believe this," she said as she stood back to survey the results of her efforts. Without soap, water and some strong stain remover, there wasn't much more she could do.

"It must be in the genes. Like mother, like son," he teased. He studied her face and added, "That was a joke, Dana. And it was an accident."

After watching her work, Cleland said, "My apologies. You all right, Dana? Sorry, Quentin. The missus keeps telling me to watch where I'm going."

"No harm done," Quentin said graciously.

"Again, I must offer to pay any dry-cleaning costs." Dana twisted her hands together.

"Why, he wouldn't dream of letting you do that. He's got more money than God," Cleland said with a laugh. Then someone from across the room called him over.

"He's right, Dana. It's not a big deal. Forget it."

"If you say so. I just can't believe the Hewitts have clobbered you twice. But I promise I won't come near you again."

"Ever?" he asked.

Was that disappointment on his face?

"Not while I've got food or drink in my hand," she qualified, trying to quell the glow his expression had caused.

"Deal," Quentin said. "But it wasn't your fault."

"Still, if this keeps up, you won't have any decent clothes left. I know how hard it is to get stains out."

"Not as hard as it's been to get you out of my thoughts," he mumbled.

"What was that?"

"I said, you should know with your tots. About stains, I mean," he added.

"You can say that again." She met his blue-eyed gaze, which held an intensity that stole the breath from her lungs. Suddenly he grinned and it was as if the heavens had opened and the earth stood still. Her heart skipped.

"From now on, I'll wear a raincoat when I'm around you," he teased.

"Go ahead. Joke about it. But truly, I feel just awful. This time, I will make it up to you."

No excuses. Time and money were hurdles she could overcome with ingenuity. Before another twenty-four hours passed, she would do something to show him how very sorry she was. The only question: how do you make amends to a man who has more money than God?

Chapter Two

The morning after the chamber of commerce meeting, Quentin entered his office and sat down behind his desk. At the same time, the intercom buzzed and he pushed the button. "Yes, Doleen?"

"You have a visitor."

"Who is it?"

"Sheriff Malone is here to see you, Mr. McCormack."

"Send him in."

Quentin figured he was making a pitch for the police department's Halloween fund. Usually one of the deputies made a phone call; it was good that the sheriff was making a personal appeal. The man kept too much to himself. And the annual event was a worthy cause. The money raised was used for a haunted house to keep the kids supervised and out of mischief. Every year, Quentin made a generous donation. After all, Storkville was all about kids.

A vision of Dana Hewitt and her three children flashed

through his mind. It was something that had been happening on an alarmingly regular basis ever since he'd met her. Even though he'd done his darnedest to forget her. It might be easier if he could put his finger on exactly what made her so unforgettable.

After seeing her again last night, sleep had been elusive. When he'd finally managed to doze off, his dreams had been of Dana. He'd never met a woman who had captivated him so quickly and so completely.

When his office door opened, Quentin was relieved that he didn't have to pursue his last thought. Then he noticed the grim look on the sheriff's face. Tucker Malone was tall, imposing and probably intimidating to someone on the wrong side of the law. His brown hair showed silver at his temples. His eyes, the color of dark chocolate, hid secrets that Quentin had a feeling were painful. Not a stretch, since he'd been an undercover detective for the Chicago police department. Quentin didn't know the sheriff well, but he liked and respected him.

He held out his hand. "Good morning, Tucker."

"Quentin," the sheriff answered, firmly clasping his outstretched hand.

"Have a seat," he said, indicating one of the leather wing chairs resting in front of his desk. Then he sat down on the other side.

"Thanks. But this isn't a social call," the sheriff answered, lowering himself into the chair.

"Oh?"

"It's about the twins abandoned at the day-care center."

Quentin had heard that the sheriff had been called in because no one had claimed the babies. Since then, Tucker had been following up every lead. But Quentin had no idea why he'd come to see him. He had no information to aid in the search.

Tucker cleared his throat. "There was a rattle found with the twins' belongings when they were left at Hannah's."

"I didn't know that."

He nodded. "Good. I've been trying to keep details quiet. Cleaner that way."

"Did it lead you to the mother?"

"No. But maybe the father." The man's piercing gaze never wavered.

Quentin tensed as he went cold inside. "What are you implying?"

Tucker pulled a long-handled, tarnished metal rattle from his shirt pocket. "I think this might belong to you. It's silver. Expensive. And has the McCormack crest on it."

"Are you sure?" Quentin asked. Stunned didn't come close to describing how he felt.

"The markings are faint so it took me a while to place it. But you'd know best." He held it out.

Quentin hesitated a moment. "Will I smudge any fingerprints?"

One corner of the sheriff's mouth turned up. "You've been watching too many cop shows on TV." He shook his head. "It was dusted for prints, but we couldn't get a clean set."

Quentin took the rattle and examined it. Several moments later anger sliced through him as he recognized the nearly worn-away family crest. What the hell was going on? "This is a McCormack heirloom, all right."

"Any idea why it was with the twins?"

He shook his head. "Not a clue."

"Would it have something to do with you being their father?" Tucker asked grimly.

"No."

"That's it?"

"I can do self-righteous indignation as well as the next guy. I could raise my voice and pound on the desk, but it wouldn't make my answer any more true. I'm responsible about that sort of thing." He remembered using almost the same words to Dana. "I'm as certain as I can be that I have not fathered any children—let alone the boy and girl left at Hannah's."

"I'd like to keep the rattle. It's still evidence," Tucker explained. Quentin handed it over. Some of the sheriff's tension seemed to ease as he took the long silver handle and replaced it in his pocket. "You didn't give the rattle to anyone?"

"No."

"Do you have any idea how it came to be with the babies?"

"No."

"Who would have access to it on the estate?"

"Everyone who comes into the house. There's a display of heirlooms in one of the bedrooms. And you've been in Storkville long enough to know that there are numerous social and charitable functions held at the McCormack estate. I'll check with my mother and see if she's noticed anything missing."

He nodded. "You do that. In the meantime, you might want to have a DNA test."

"But I—"

"If you're innocent, Quentin, you have nothing to worry about. Why not take steps to clear your name? It's the only way to be sure."

The man had a point. "I'll call the lab and make an appointment."

Tucker stood up. "Good." He went to the door, and started to turn the knob. "Quentin?"

"Sheriff?"

"I just want you to know that I'm keeping this investigation as quiet as I can."

"Thanks, Tucker."

"I'm not doing it for you. I don't want this case compromised by publicity. If it's the last thing I do, I *will* find out who those kids belong to." His voice was laced with anger and something that felt like regret.

Then he was gone.

Quentin ran his hand through his hair. In spite of his own denials, he realized that there was a good chance the sheriff believed he had abandoned those babies. If he was ever lucky enough to have children, no way would he turn his back on them. Still, it was a good thing he'd made his donation to Hannah's day-care center anonymously. That information, along with the rattle, would probably convince Storkville's lawman that he was guilty beyond a doubt.

He didn't care what Tucker Malone thought. But if Dana Hewitt heard of the suspicions regarding him, what would she think? Nothing good, he figured. And he realized he wanted her favorable opinion. He picked up the phone. One DNA test ASAP.

After hours, Quentin looked out his office window. The day had started out with a visit from the sheriff and had gone downhill from there. He was glad it was over.

He studied the lights in businesses up and down Main Street. He could almost see Bassinets & Booties from here. A vision filled his head: mahogany hair, gray eyes, full lips. Dana. A beautiful name for a beautiful woman he'd tried to forget after their first meeting.

"Mission impossible," he said ruefully.

Since their encounter the previous evening, his thoughts of Dana had heated up. And not just because she'd baptized him with the contents of her coffee cup. He'd spent a restless night dreaming of running his hands through her hair, kissing her until they both went up in flames. His intercom buzzed, startling him.

He swiveled his chair away from the window and answered. "Yes, Doleen?"

"You have a visitor."

He wasn't expecting anyone. This was the way his day had started. He groaned. Not Sheriff Malone again. Since he wasn't the babies' father, what more could there be to talk about? His stomach knotted when he remembered his own secret. Had Tucker discovered that he was the day-care center's anonymous benefactor?

"Who is it?" he demanded, dreading the answer.

"A woman and three adorable children," Doleen answered, a smile in her voice.

Dana and her kids, he thought. He'd tried all day to shake his dismal mood. Now he was as excited as a teenage boy going to the prom with the most popular girl in school.

"Send them in," he said.

A moment later, his office door opened and Lukie raced toward him. Quentin stood in front of his desk and braced himself for impact. He bent down and lifted the little guy into his arms.

"Hi, Lukie."

"Hi, Mr. Mac."

They grinned at each other. Then he saw Dana, standing in the doorway with Molly and Kelly. He drank in the sight of her like the plains soak up the first rain after a drought. He could hardly breathe. If anything, she grew more beautiful every time he saw her.

He looked closer and noticed that her eyes lacked their special sparkle. Her full mouth turned up in a smile of greeting, but he knew it was the generic one she used for customers at the end of a particularly long day. She seemed tired, or tense. Or both.

"Hello, Dana," he said. Then to the two girls now clinging to her legs, "Hi, Kelly. Hi, Molly. Thanks for coming to see me."

Shyly, they hid their faces in their mother's red dress, but in such a way that they could peek at him.

"You remembered their names," Dana said. This time her smile was genuine and for just a moment her eyes shone.

"Of course." He tried to sound casual, but inside he was doing the touchdown dance at pleasing her. "Although they look so identical, I'd crash and burn if you asked me to address them by name *and* be correct."

She laughed. "When they were born, I knew that would be a problem. So I came up with a cheat sheet. Molly has a small mole, or beauty mark as I refer to it, just to the right of her mouth. *M* for Molly and mole."

"Clever mother," he said.

"Thank you. One tries even if one isn't always successful." There was an edge to her voice that made him suspect a double meaning to her words. And another black look replaced the pleasure on her face. "But I didn't barge in to dazzle you with my foxy maternal instincts."

She just dazzled him with her foxy self, he thought. Then he noticed the basket in her hands and remembered her promise to make retribution for dumping coffee on him. He wanted to tell her she could dump as often as she wanted if it meant he could spend time with her. He realized that he very much wanted to do that.

"Why *did* you drop in and dazzle me?" he asked instead.

She smiled. "If you'll put my son down, we'll do our thing."

"There you go, big guy," he said, setting the boy on the rug.

He raced over to his mom, and Quentin realized Lukas had only one pace: light speed. Dana bent down and together they moved forward and handed him the green-cellophane-wrapped basket.

"For you," Lukie said proudly. "Cuz me and mommy spilled."

"Thank you." Quentin took the basket. At the same time, he got a whiff of Dana's fragrance and realized he could find her in a pitch-black room. The memory of her scent would haunt him forever.

The thought made him hot all over. In his shaky hands, the cellophane snapped, crackled and popped. Not unlike what was going on inside him. Could she tell? He glanced at her to see if she'd noticed.

But she was watching Lukie, who had lost interest in the peace offering. The boy had crawled under his desk and was now on the other side diddling with his computer keyboard.

"Lukie, don't touch Mr. Mac's things," she warned him.

"Okay," he said and stopped. For a moment.

"I should have left them with Hannah for a few more minutes while I made my peace offering," she said. "But they're there all day and I hate to leave them longer than I absolutely must."

"I'm glad you didn't. I like seeing them. And this is great," Quentin said, peering at the wrapping. It was not quite transparent enough to see the contents. "But you really didn't have to do it."

"It's no big deal. But do you have any idea how hard it is to come up with a contrition offering for a man who has more money than God?"

As always, his warning signals went up at the mention of his money. "It's the thought that counts," he said automatically.

"That's a cliché, but I hope you really mean it," she answered.

"Open your pwesent," Lukie said. He raced around the desk. "Mommy and me wapped it. Me and my sisters maked cookies."

"Way to go, buddy." Quentin looked at the boy's mother. "When did you have time?"

She shrugged. "They get up at the crack of dawn. We baked this morning before work and day care."

Quentin put the basket on his desk and untied the ribbon. Inside he found cookies, muffins and peanut brittle. Nestled in the center of the baked goods there was an envelope. He opened it and found a gift certificate to the local dry cleaner.

"Perfect," he said chuckling. He met Dana's gaze. "Thank you."

"You're welcome," she said.

The children lost interest as soon as the basket was opened and they drifted away. Quentin noticed the girls quietly checking out the magazines sitting on the table in the corner.

"Don't touch things," Dana warned them. "You too, Lukie. Put down Mr. Mac's eyeglasses." The boy had retreated to the other side of his desk again and was examining the glasses Quentin used for computer work.

Quentin studied Dana. She was definitely tense. He hoped she wasn't really worried about spilling on him. Or was something else bothering her?

"The kids are fine, Dana. It's their job to explore," he said gently.

"And it's my job to pay for what they destroy in the process of doing their job," she said. Glancing around his office she continued, "And you have a wonderful office with all kinds of things to break."

"Thank you, I think."

"So much to explore, so little time," she said, giving his work space an admiring glance.

He followed her gaze. He liked it and was pleased that she approved. On the hunter-green carpet, his oak desk and computer return filled the center of the room. Across from it was the soft brown leather sofa. From time to time, he had picked out pieces of art and knick-knacks that caught his fancy. The cost hadn't fazed him.

A worried frown marred her smooth forehead. "But do you have something against plastic?"

"Excuse me?"

"Everything in here is breakable. I'd better get the children home before you regret that we dropped in. *Dropped* being the operative word."

"Don't go yet," he said before he could stop himself. "The carpet is thick. Things bounce."

"I'm glad. Because my budget doesn't have much bounce," she said ruefully. "But we're doing fine financially," she added quickly.

To reassure her or himself, he wondered. He decided to change the subject. "How's business?"

"Good. Storkville is a wonderful community for a

baby store. The population is growing steadily, hence the store is doing well. I think word is out about what a great place it is to raise children.'' Her pretty face clouded. ''Which is probably why the twins were left with Hannah. I hope they find whoever abandoned those babies.''

''I couldn't agree more,'' he said, uncomfortable with the direction his change of subject had taken her.

''There should be a special place in hell for someone like that. Who could walk out on their children? Steffie and Sammy are so adorable. I worry about Molly, Kelly and Lukie every moment I'm not with them.''

Had she heard that the sheriff suspected him of fathering the twins? He studied her reaction, trying to decide if her tirade was general or specific to him. Suddenly an alarmed expression suffused her features and she hurried around his desk.

''Lukie, put that down,'' she said, removing a ceramic paperweight from the child's hand. She glanced ruefully at Quentin. ''Something tells me you don't do much business with three-year-olds.''

He laughed. ''No. But I'm looking into it.''

He realized he wasn't joking. The moment she'd walked into his office with her munchkin marauders, their energy and innocent curiosity had lifted his spirits. He liked watching them. He liked watching her. He would like to have them around. A lot.

He wondered if Aunt Gertie's lemonade, which he'd sipped the night before, was to blame for his thoughts. The rumor was that it was supposed to help women get pregnant. Could it put thoughts of settling down with a ready-made family into a lonely bachelor's head? Even one who had been avoiding gold diggers all his adult life?

Did Dana fall into the gold digger category? His every instinct said no. She had ignored him after their first meeting. His gut told him she wouldn't be here now if not for the lucky coffee accident last night. And she'd had a little help from the mayor. He made a mental note to send Cleland Knox a special greeting when the holidays rolled around this year.

With her son's hand firmly gripped in her own, Dana walked back around in front of him. "If your clientele expands to children, I'd advise you to kid-proof your office. Otherwise the pressure will age you before your time."

"I'm not worried. Relax, Dana. They're things. Replaceable."

"Easy for you to say," she said, sighing loudly as Lukie pulled his hand from hers and wiggled back under the desk. Looking over her shoulder, she saw Kelly and Molly touching a crystal bell on a shelf in the curio cabinet in the corner.

"Put that down, girls," she said, an edge to her voice. "Please don't touch."

"But, Mommy," Kelly said.

"It's pretty," her sister continued as if she was finishing the thought. "When the light shines it makes wed, and bwue."

"Me see," Lukie said, quickly moving beside them.

"No, Lukie." Dana started toward the trio. "Don't touch it."

"Wanna see," he said.

He grabbed it. When he turned toward the light, the delicate handle hit the shelf and broke off. Then he dropped the bell and it shattered against the base of the cabinet.

"Oh," Dana said. "Oh, no."

Quentin stepped in. He gently moved the children away from the broken glass. "Don't touch," he warned quietly. "The pieces are sharp. They can cut you. Are you all okay?" They nodded, but he scanned them quickly and didn't see any blood, so he figured no one had been hit by flying glass.

Lukie stared up at him with a contrite expression that looked awfully familiar. "Sorry, Mr. Mac."

"Accidents happen, buddy." He stooped and picked up the pieces of crystal.

When he met Dana's gaze, he realized she was more fragile than the bell. Her gray eyes shimmered. "I'll bet that cost at least as much as my monthly grocery bill," she said.

Close, he thought. But how did she know its value? If she was on a tight budget, would she have any idea what the replacement price was?

She bent and took Lukie's arm. "Son, that was a no-no. I asked you not to touch Mr. Mac's things. No cartoons after supper," she said sternly. "Straight to bed."

"No, Mommy." The little boy's mouth quivered. Then he started to cry.

The next thing Quentin knew, Molly and Kelly were sobbing. Dana looked at him helplessly. "I'm so sorry. Somehow, I'll make it up to you. I wonder how many cookies I'll have to bake. I—I have to g-go—"

"Don't cry, Dana." Quentin moved toward her and reached out a hand to comfort her.

She backed away. "Please don't touch me. I have just about enough self-control to make it home with the triplets before I lose it. But if you're nice to me, that time frame c-could be c-considerably shorter."

He pulled her into his arms and felt her body shake. He heard a sob before she put a hand over her mouth.

"M-mommy? Sorry, Mommy. Don't cwy," Lukie said, burying his face in his mother's leg. The girls followed suit.

Group hug? Quentin thought ruefully. He disengaged himself from the crying quartet and pressed the intercom for his secretary.

"Yes?"

"Doleen, I could use your assistance."

"Right away."

The next moment his door opened and super-efficient Doleen Powell walked in. Short, brunette, and wearing wire-rimmed spectacles, she was a bundle of energy. "How can I help, Quentin?"

"What would it take to coax the children into your office?" he asked.

"Food." She glanced at her watch and nodded. "It's after six. They're probably hungry and tired. Can't do anything about bedtime, but I could call for a pizza."

"Pizza?" Lukie said, anticipation chasing the tears from his eyes.

"I like pizza," Molly said. Kelly nodded enthusiastically.

Doleen smiled. "Do I know kids or what?"

"There will be something special in your Christmas bonus this year," Quentin said more grateful than he could say.

"There always is, boss," she answered. She looked at the kids. "You guys want to help me call for the pizza?" When they nodded, she held her arm out toward the door and said, "Come into my office."

The three children ran to the door. As she ushered them through it, Doleen said, "Your mom is going to talk to Mr. McCormack for a few minutes while we have pizza in here. Is that okay with you guys?"

"Yay," they said together just before the door closed.

Quentin looked at Dana. Tears streaked her face. Red rimmed her eyes. She sniffled loudly. And God help him, she'd never looked more beautiful. He went to her and pulled her back into his arms. Sobs shook her.

"I—I warned you not to touch me."

"No guts no glory," he said as lightly as he could with his heart beating like crazy. She felt so delicate, so fragile—so soft, so warm. Completely wonderful. He didn't know how, but he knew this breakdown was not her style.

Her tears dampened the front of his blue dress shirt. "There's never a raincoat around when you need one."

"Not again," she said trying to pull away.

"That was a joke, Dana. Lighten up. Cut yourself some slack. You're a single mom. Three kids would be a handful for *two* parents."

Instead of helping, his words sent her into another crying spell. He wrapped his arms around her and held her close. He rubbed her back and whispered meaningless words meant to comfort and reassure.

When she was finally quiet against him, except for an occasional hiccup, he said, "Now, I think it's time you told me what's really going on."

Chapter Three

Dana had never been so mortified in her life. Breaking down like that! Quentin must think she was a raving lunatic. And she couldn't blame him. But, God help her, she didn't want him to think that. Maybe there was a way to salvage the situation.

"What makes you think there's something going on?" she hedged.

She backed away from him and reached into the pocket of her dress for a tissue. A mother of three always had one.

"You're not the kind of woman who breaks down like this. It's not your style."

He was right. But how did he know that? She'd been with her husband over three years and he'd never realized that about her. The last time they'd talked, he'd told her to stop with the tears. A classic female manipulation, he'd called it even though he'd never seen *her* cry more than once or twice.

"How do you know what my style is?" she asked curiously. "After all, we barely know each other."

"I size people up pretty quickly. The day Lukie got away from you, you were anxious and frantic. But not—" he met her gaze "—hysterical. This is not your usual unflappable style," he said again.

He stuck his hands in the pockets of his navy pinstripe slacks as he met her gaze. Her tears had blotched his powder-blue shirt, reminding her that he'd held her while she cried. No man had ever held her while she cried. He'd been nothing but kind since they'd met. Correction, kind and sexy. And he was entitled to the same treatment—the kind part, not the sexy. It was her attraction to him that had made her words sharper than she'd intended. She didn't want to be attracted to him, or any other man.

As much as she'd tried to tell herself that she wasn't attracted, her body shivered, shuddered or sizzled just because he smiled, spoke or sized her up in his charming, devastating way. But that was her problem and certainly no excuse for her behavior.

He deserved an explanation. She sighed. "You're right, Quentin. There is something wrong."

He reached out a hand and curved his strong, lean fingers around her elbow. "Let's sit down over here and you can tell me about it," he said leading her to the sofa.

His touch discharged sparks of warmth through her and made her legs as weak as a newborn colt's. With an effort, she pulled herself together. She would not humiliate herself further by collapsing at his feet.

He saw her to the leather couch and she lowered herself onto the supple cushion, then stifled a sigh of appreciation. Why should it surprise her that it was soft and comforting like everything else in his office? Like Quentin himself. It was also expensive. She'd lived with Jeff Hewitt long enough to know quality when she sat on it, and this was about as quality as it came. Thank goodness the children would be eating their pizza anywhere but here. But she completely trusted his secretary to watch over them. Probably because the woman worked for Quentin aka Sir Galahad.

She met his expectant gaze and wondered where to start her explanations. Best to jump in with both feet, she decided. She sat up straighter. "My husband's parents are threatening legal action to take the children away from me."

"What?" His deep voice wrapped around that one word and vibrated with anger. "Why?"

"For starters, they never approved of me. My background and upbringing was very different from their son's. Jeff came from money and social position. I was raised in a blue-collar, working-class family. There was lots of love but not much money."

"There's nothing wrong with that," he answered.

Dana thought a wary look flickered in his blue eyes, but then it was gone. She continued, "I'm proud of who I am, where I came from. It makes me sad that my parents didn't live long enough to know my children. Especially since the Hewitts have never accepted me."

"It's their loss."

"It'll be mine," she said, trying to keep her voice steady. "Unless I can convince them to leave me and the kids alone."

"It explains a lot. Like why you were so outspoken about the abandoned twins."

She nodded. "I'm facing the possibility of losing my children, my life," she whispered, "and someone just walked out on Sammy and Steffie.'' She shook her head. ''It's inconceivable to me how anyone could do that. It's been weeks, and no word—'' She stopped as emotion choked her.

''I don't understand how your in-laws could do anything.'' Something flickered in his eyes as he changed the subject back to her problem. ''No court in the country would take the triplets from you. You're a loving, caring mother.''

''Thanks,'' she said, his praise filling up a hollow place inside her. ''But they're wealthy. I'm afraid if they pour enough money into the fight, they can do whatever they want. I don't have enough to hire an attorney, let alone put up more than token resistance. So far it's just talk. But—'' She stopped and caught her top lip between her teeth.

''Tell me what they're saying.''

''That I'm a single parent with three children. That I came from nothing and that hasn't changed.''

His mouth twisted, telling her that he disagreed with her words. ''What about your husband's life insurance?''

''There wasn't any.'' When an angry scowl took hold of his features and he opened his mouth, she held up her hand. ''It's a long, sad story. Don't ask. The point is, I don't have much money.''

''Lots of people raise families on limited incomes. It's not grounds for removing the children.''

''They criticize the fact that I have to work full-time to provide for myself and the kids. Lukie and Kelly and Molly are being raised by strangers who can't give them the time they need. Or bring them up as Hewitts should be.''

''Again, lots of families are in the same boat. Two-income households are a fact of life in this country. That's why day-care centers like Hannah's are so vital.''

''I agree,'' she said. She tried to suppress her shiver of excitement at his passionate support and was dismally unsuccessful. His outspoken championing of children was so appealing. It made her want his arms around her again. But not just for comfort. She had the most absurd desire to know what his lips would feel like against her own. With an effort she said, ''But all the Hewitts can see is that their grandchildren are being raised by their inferiors.''

''That's ridiculous.''

''I tried to get them to come to Storkville and see for themselves what the town is like. I urged them to meet Hannah and her staff, as well as the volunteers at BabyCare, so they would be reassured that the triplets' environment is safe and nurturing. I suggested that the situation is a good thing, that meeting different people will make them well-rounded individuals. Many people have a lot to offer them.''

''And?''

''They hung up on me. The last thing they said is that I'd be hearing from their lawyer.''

He took her hand in his large warm one. ''I'm really sorry, Dana. What can I—''

''Oh, before the lawyer threat, they said it's not safe for one woman to raise three kids without a husband. It's dangerous, because they're a handful.''

He shook his head. ''Almost my exact words a few moments ago. No wonder you lost it. I'm sorry. I was trying to make you feel better. Instead, I practically paraphrased your in-laws.''

''There's no way you could have known. They're adamant that the children would be better off with them.

It's a household where money is no object and there would be a mother and father.''

''Father?'' he said. He said the one word thoughtfully and almost to himself.

Dana could almost see the wheels in his mind spinning. His eyes shone with an inner excitement. What in the world was he thinking?

She knew she should take her hand from his, but she couldn't bear to relinquish the warmth, the support, the connection. It felt so wonderful, as if she wasn't alone. Although she knew that was silly. She was in the fight of her life and she had no one in her corner. She was more grateful than she could say that he'd listened as she unburdened herself.

''Quentin, if I thought for a moment that the children would be happy with them and thrive in that environment, I would give them my blessing. But I know them. George and Beatrice Hewitt are narrow-minded and selfish. They would pawn the kids off on servants. The triplets would be so lonely in that sophisticated, adult atmosphere. It's not a place for children. It's too adult. It's like—'' she stopped searching for an example.

''My office?'' he offered wryly.

In spite of her worries, she couldn't help smiling. It felt good and she was grateful to him for pulling it out of her. ''No,'' she denied. ''This is a warm atmosphere that just happens to be filled with breakables.''

His grin was fleeting. ''You can't let them win, Dana.''

''I won't,'' she said firmly. ''But part of me worries that they've got a point. To someone who doesn't look deeper, they appear to be the salt of the earth. Worse, they're something I can't be. A mother *and* father.''

He stood up suddenly and Dana missed his warmth

beside her. He stuck his hands in his pockets and started to pace.

''Quentin?''

He didn't seem to hear her. He kept walking and occasionally ran his fingers through his hair.

''Quentin? What is it?''

He turned to her and there was an intensity in his expression that she found thrilling. Not to mention sexy as all get-out. ''Quentin, say something. I don't know what to do.''

''Marry me.''

In her whole life, Dana had never been on the receiving end of a jaw-dropping remark. But the two words made her jaw drop. She was completely speechless.

With hands on his hips, he stood in front of her and stared down. ''What do you say?''

She shrugged, shook her head in disbelief, and extended her hands in a helpless gesture.

''C'mon, Dana. It's easy. There's just one three-letter word I want to hear.''

''Why?'' she asked, her voice a whisper.

''That's not the right one. But the question is valid.'' He took a deep breath. ''It's the answer to both our problems.''

''I thought I was the only one with a problem.''

Shaking his head, he said, ''Lady, I could give you an earful about problems. For starters, having a wife would be practical for me. I'm the president of the company and it would be sensible for business and society functions. A settled CEO helps stabilize stock prices. Our investors don't trust uncertainty.''

He had an odd look on his face, as if something else was troubling him.

''I could shoot that full of holes, Quentin. But let's

say for a moment that I buy it, what would marriage do for me?''

"I could give you and the kids security."

She stood up. "I'm not a charity case, Quentin. I can take care of my children."

"Under normal circumstances, yes. But you said yourself that the Hewitts have the money to win a custody case. I'm offering to put all my considerable resources at your disposal."

"And I repeat, what do you get out of it?" She met his gaze. "A man who looks like— I mean, a man like you could get any woman he wants to hostess a business or social function. Why tie yourself down—legally speaking? Especially to a woman with triplets?"

"I like the kids. And I like you."

"Be still my heart."

"This is no time for flowery, romantic declarations. From the first day we met I liked you. And that's the honest truth."

She studied his expression—his eyes. All she saw was sincerity. But Jeff had seemed sincere, too. Right up until she'd found lipstick on his collar that wasn't hers. His deception had been exceedingly painful.

"I like the truth. But marriage?" she asked.

"Think about it. I have a law firm on retainer. Most of the time they twiddle their thumbs. Look on the bright side. I would finally be getting something for my money."

"But marriage?"

"If this thing goes to court, you would have the best. You would have a husband and father for the kids. Who would look better to a judge than their own mother and her husband?"

"But marriage?"

"It's not skydiving over the Grand Canyon, for Pete's sake. It's a win-win situation for both of us. There are no hidden dangers."

Easy for him to say. He'd never been married. But her marriage had taken the stars from her eyes forever. She'd been completely disillusioned. "I still don't understand what you would win. Seems an awfully drastic way to get yourself a hostess."

"Drastic situations call for bold measures." He ran his hand through his hair. "Okay. How about this? You could run interference for me with women who are only interested in me for my money."

"Is that a problem?"

"If you only knew."

Before she could respond, the phone buzzed. He walked over to the desk and pushed the button. "Yes, Doleen?"

"The hospital lab phoned to confirm your appointment tomorrow morning at eight."

"Thanks. Are the kids okay?"

"Chowing down pizza, and good as gold."

"How are you?"

"Watching them chow down pizza and loving it," she answered, then clicked off.

Knowing the children were happy, Dana relaxed. But what was that about the hospital? He looked fine—better than fine. But she realized that she was concerned about him. "You're not ill, are you?"

"No. DNA test," he murmured.

"DNA? Why?" she asked distractedly.

"Like all the other men in town, to rule out paternity of the twins."

She couldn't say why, but she had a feeling there was

more he wasn't saying. Before she could pursue it he asked her a question.

"So, what do you think about getting married? To save my virtue," he added.

"How do you know I'm not after your money? After all, I've been accused of that before."

"By your in-laws."

She nodded. "They don't pull punches."

"Neither do I. And to answer your question, I have no idea whether or not you're interested in my money. But I've seen firsthand your devotion to your children. And since I initiated the proposal, I'm in control of the situation."

It was her turn to wince. At his phrasing. Control. She'd had her fill. From Jeff. Now his parents. She liked Quentin. More than she should. In a very short time, he'd found his way into her dreams at night and her thoughts during the day. If this went any further, she would be vulnerable to him. That would never do. Not again.

Before she answered him, she took a deep cleansing breath. "Thank you, Quentin. Your offer is kind—very generous, in fact. And nine out of ten women would think I've lost my mind. But my answer has to be no. Even with a prenuptial agreement to prove that I'm not after your money, it would be a mistake for both of us."

"How can you know that?"

"For one simple reason—I don't want to get married again."

"I'm sorry to hear that."

"Me too." She looked at her watch. "Look at the time. I didn't mean to keep you so late. I need to get the children home." She walked to the door and looked back at him.

''You won't reconsider?''

She knew he meant the marriage proposal. ''It has nothing to do with you, Quentin. It has to do with love. That's the only reason to get married. And there's no way that will ever happen to me again.''

Dana sat in her office upstairs at Bassinets and Booties. It was lunchtime and she unwrapped her tuna sandwich on her desk.

She thought about Quentin McCormack. Less than twenty-four hours ago, he'd asked her to marry him. The memory was surreal. She could hardly believe it had actually happened. But a more pressing question: why had she broken down like that and bared her soul?

''He's a man whose niceness invites women to get up close and personal and he doesn't seem to mind a bit of hysteria tossed into the mix,'' she mused, taking a bite of her sandwich. He was more than that.

A vision of his strong, square jaw, well-formed nose, and piercing blue eyes invaded her mind. Her heart thumped and it was a good thing she was already sitting. Images of the good-looking ''Mr. Mac'' always made her knees weak, so she tried to keep him out of her thoughts. But after his proposal, that was like trying to stop a speeding locomotive by standing on the track.

There was a knock on her door. ''Come in,'' she called.

Sally Smith, one of her salesclerks, entered the room. She was a short, plump, hazel-eyed redhead. ''Dana, sorry to bother you at lunch. But there's a lady who insists on seeing you.''

''That's all right,'' Dana said, putting down her sandwich. She wasn't hungry anyway. ''Send her in.''

"Right this way," Sally said, looking over her shoulder at someone in the hall.

When the clerk backed away, a tall brunette entered the room. "Mrs. Dana Hewitt?"

"That's me. May I help you with something?"

The woman pulled an envelope out of her purse, put it on the desk, and quickly backed away. "This is a summons."

Dana went cold and her hands started to shake. "What is this about?" As if she didn't know. Panic welled up inside her.

The woman shrugged. "My job is to deliver it. But you might want to get an attorney. Have a nice day."

When Dana looked up, she was gone. She glanced down at the envelope, the return address written in black—dark black. The word *court* caught her attention. That was very bad. She trembled from head to toe and could hardly draw breath into her lungs as she opened the letter. Her chest ached as the words *Hewitt vs Hewitt, custody hearing* and a date in January danced before her eyes.

"Oh, God, they've done it," she gasped, trying to catch her breath. "They're suing me for custody of my children."

She needed the best attorney money could hire. But she hadn't the money to pay a first-year law student, she thought desperately. What was she going to do?

She remembered Quentin saying his legal staff had very little to keep them busy and it would be a favor if she put them to work. Why had she turned down his proposal? But she knew the answer. She hadn't really believed the Hewitts would take legal action. So why would Quentin help her now? Even nice men had their limits.

But she had no one else to turn to.

She pushed aside her lunch and stood, a woman with a mission. "Quentin, I hope you understand that it's a woman's prerogative to change her mind."

Quentin's intercom buzzed while he was on the phone with a client. He put his caller on hold to answer. "Doleen, I thought I told you—"

"I know you didn't want to see anyone, Quentin. But you've been in a lousy mood all morning. There's someone here to snap you out of it. So no matter what you say, I'm sending her in."

"But—" The line went dead, and Quentin made a mental note to adjust Doleen's Christmas bonus accordingly.

Then it sank in. Her?

His heart rate kicked up like an unexpected rally on the New York stock exchange. Then his door opened and Dana Hewitt walked in. His first thought was how glad he was to see her. Then he noticed her pale face and trembling lips.

He took the caller off hold. "Sam, can I get back to you later?" When he received an affirmative, he hung up.

He stood and rounded his desk. "What can I do for you?"

"Marry me," she said breathlessly.

Of all the things he might have expected, that one had never entered his mind. Something had happened to send her to him. Her cheeks were red, attesting to her hurrying up the street to his office. The weather had turned cold and she hadn't bothered with a sweater or coat. Her mouth trembled and she was shaking like a leaf.

"Would you like some coffee?" he asked.

"No, thanks."

He took her arm and led her to the sofa. Sitting beside her, he ignored the heat flash produced by the brush of her nylon-clad knee against his. This wasn't the time. And she'd made it clear yesterday that she was still carrying a torch for the husband she'd lost. The thought produced an unexpected tightness in his chest.

She looked at him. "It wasn't necessary for you to cut short your business call."

"It can wait." His words produced an unexpected wavery smile that tugged at his heart.

"I can't remember the last time, if ever, anyone put something aside for me."

"Not even your husband?" After the words were out, he wished he could call them back. Or better yet, rewind and start over, this time with a gag in his mouth.

"No." Her shoulders sagged, and her fingers worried the material of her dress across her knees.

"What's wrong?" he asked again. "Yesterday you made it clear that you didn't want to get married again."

She shrugged. "I've had time to think about it."

So had he. All night, as a matter of fact. He'd thought about little else but her. He admired her pride and devotion to her children. He respected her independence and determination to take care of her family. He'd realized how much he'd wanted to be a part of it—especially *after* her rejection. Which reminded him of her parting words.

His heart hammered in his chest as he took a deep breath. "What about love?"

"It's the reason I'm here."

Chapter Four

"You're saying you love me?" Quentin asked skeptically.

He'd been willing to marry her without bringing love into it. Was she trying to impress him? Was she, after all, like the other women who just wanted his money? The beginnings of disillusionment brought him down. He'd begun to think she was the exception. Because of his own background, was he just a sucker for a struggling single mom?

Clear gray eyes looked into his own. "To quote someone I know and respect," she said softly but firmly, "this is no time for flowery, romantic declarations."

He was more put out by the word *respect* than the fact that she'd thrown his own words back at him. He could live with being described as the man who lusted after her, or the fella who had trouble keeping his hands off her, or even the guy with a world-class butt. But respect? He might as well be her brother.

An effective reminder not to count on anything deeper

between them. This was about her husband. If she hadn't gotten over the guy in almost a year, it certainly wasn't going to happen overnight with him. And very possibly not at all. Get real, McCormack.

And why did he even want that? Because she was beautiful, bright and funny. And because he couldn't shake the feeling that she *was* different, that money wasn't the most important thing to her.

"I don't get it," he said, shaking his head. "If love is the only reason to get married, why are you here?"

"I love my children," she said simply.

Of course. It was about the kids. He should have known right away. But somehow his mental capacity seemed to go on the blink whenever he was this close to Dana Hewitt. The heat she generated in him caused static that threatened to short-circuit every one of his brain cells.

She pulled an envelope from the pocket of her denim jumper and handed it to him. "Look at this, Quentin."

He scanned the contents, then met her worried gaze as he reached over and squeezed her hand reassuringly. The summons explained everything.

"I never thought they would go through with it. Not really." She looked miserable. "I have nowhere else to turn. Without your help, I'm afraid I could actually lose my children. Quentin, I'm hoping that you'll allow me to reconsider and accept your proposal."

He wondered how he could be so angry at the same time he felt like he'd just found the number-one item on his wish list under the Christmas tree. It didn't matter that she'd only come to him because she was desperate to keep her children. It didn't matter that a wife and family would help with damage control when it got out that he was suspected of being the abandoned twins' father. It only mattered that she'd said yes.

"The offer is still on the table," he said, trying to sound casual.

"Good."

A great weight lifted from Dana. She let out the breath she hadn't realized she'd been holding. The threat had been hanging over her ever since she'd moved to Storkville. It was a tremendous relief to know she wasn't in this alone anymore. That opened a floodgate of other feelings. Top of the heap was wrenching loneliness. Now that she had an ally, she felt the heavy weight of the burden she'd been carrying so long by herself. The prospect of someone to lean on appealed to her enormously. The fact that the someone was Quentin made it even better. Get a grip, she warned herself. Today gratitude, tomorrow love?

It would be so easy to fall. Correction, it would be easy if her ability to fall in love hadn't died. But it couldn't hurt to take precautionary measures, and she had some points to clarify.

"So you still want to marry me?" she asked, making sure she was clear on the offer.

He leaned forward and rested his elbows on his knees. "Dana, I want you to know that you don't have to marry me for my help. I'll make my legal team available to you because it's the right thing to do. I would never put you in a position where you had to sacrifice yourself for your kids."

His generosity brought tears to her eyes. Sir Galahad again. What had she ever done to deserve a Quentin McCormack in her life?

"That is the sweetest thing anyone's ever said to me," she declared, blinking furiously to dry her tears.

"I mean it. What your in-laws are trying to do is wrong."

"But this is business. And everything you said last night is right. Our arrangement would not be just about legal counsel. It's about common sense. Not that the legal system has ever been accused of being fair *and* practical," she added wryly. "But if this actually goes to court, my position becomes much stronger if I'm married."

"I agree. And the sooner the better," he said.

"Why?"

"If it gets as far as court, the longer we're a married couple, the better it looks. You don't want anyone to suspect that it's a marriage of convenience—just to keep the kids."

"Even though it is," she reminded him pointedly. "And you get the stability of a family for business reasons."

"Right." His mouth pulled tight for a moment. But then he said, "So when do you think we should tie the knot?"

There were some things she wanted spelled out first. It was time to crunch numbers—or get to the bottom line. He'd used business terminology. So would she. It was better that way. If this was just business, how could either of them get hurt?

"Before we go any further, there are a couple of issues I'd like to negotiate."

"Okay." One corner of his mouth turned up.

"Don't laugh, Quentin. This is serious."

"I know. And I'm not laughing."

"Right," she said skeptically. "I actually have three simple things. Number one, the marriage will be in name only. If that's a problem for you, it's a deal-breaker for me," she said firmly.

She studied him carefully to make sure he understood what she was saying. A slight narrowing of his eyes told her that he'd gotten the message that they would have separate bedrooms.

"Okay. What's issue number two?" he asked, his voice a tad deeper than his usual tie-her-stomach-in-knots tone. The timbre tied her so tight, she wondered if she would ever feel "usual" around him again.

He was so overwhelmingly male that she lost her train of thought. Swallowing hard, she pulled herself together. "I think we should agree on a specific length of time to stay together. Say six months."

He frowned and shook his head. "This is the weirdest business deal I've ever been involved in. By definition, you don't normally discuss a merger in terms of splitting up in six months."

Her chest felt tight. This was important to her. When she'd married Jeff Hewitt, it had been with the conviction that it would be forever. His infidelity had changed everything. She needed an escape clause. She needed to know she could walk away. She needed a guarantee that she wouldn't get hurt again.

"This isn't up for discussion," she said, holding her breath as he thought it over.

"What if the custody battle drags on longer than we expect?"

His use of "we" made her glow inside. But she couldn't afford to get swept away on a wave of emotion like the last time she'd married. No one could accuse her of not learning from her mistakes.

"If that happens, we can extend our arrangement for

another six months. That's as flexible as I'm prepared to be."

He nodded, but the tightness around his mouth told her he didn't like it. "And issue number three?"

"I want a prenuptial agreement."

He straightened, his casual pose suddenly vanishing. She suspected he wasn't the sort of man who surprised easily. But there was no mistaking the fact that she'd shocked his socks off.

"I don't get it," he said, intensity darkening his already vivid blue eyes. "You've already told me you don't have any assets. Why do you want a prenup?"

"To protect *your* assets," she said firmly.

Not the least of which were his broad chest, chiseled jaw and those amazing eyes, staring at her now as if he could see into her soul. And she only hoped her three-point plan could protect her from those assets. As much as she wished he would pull her into his arms and let nature take its course, she couldn't let that happen. She had to keep her distance. Her heart was damaged goods. She no longer believed in happily-ever-after. If it were up to her she would run far and fast in the other direction. Quentin deserved someone who could truly care about him. But right now, she had to think about her children.

She cleared her throat. "I don't want anything from you except your assistance in keeping my children. You told me that it will be my job to protect you from women who only see dollar signs instead of your beautiful baby blues." That sent a shiver of awareness through her. Why now did she have to become so acutely aware that he really did have the most extraordinary eyes? But she had to ignore everything wonderful about him and keep this strictly business.

"Dana, I didn't mean *you* were after my money. If you recall, I was the one who suggested this marriage in the first place."

"Still, I take my responsibility seriously. In the spirit of my new job, I'll start by protecting you from me. I'd like your legal team to stop twiddling their thumbs and get to work drawing up an agreement stating that I want nothing from you when we split up."

He frowned and she wasn't sure if it was at the word "when" or "split."

He shook his head. "I can't decide whether or not you would take the corporate world by storm or be crushed like a grape."

"Why?" she asked.

"I've always found business to involve a lot of give-and-take. Each and every one of your points is non-negotiable."

She smiled a little sheepishly. "I'm sorry. But I feel strongly about all of them. And it's for your sake as much as mine," she added.

"Should I be miffed that an amateur negotiator has backed me against the wall, or thank you for thinking of everything?"

"I just tried to circumvent potential problems."

The expression in his eyes said he could look out for himself just fine. But all he said was, "I'll have my lawyers get to work on it right away. As well as the necessary paperwork for the marriage."

"All right."

"Now I have an issue, and it's not negotiable."

Oh, no, she thought, her stomach clenching. Just when she'd thought everything was going to be fine. When would she learn that if it looked too good to be true, it probably was?

"What is it?" she asked, bracing herself for the worst.

"I want you and the children to move into the estate with me."

She'd been so preoccupied with the terms of her plan, she hadn't given any consideration to actually living with him. Her mind raced now. As much as she hated making a decision on the spot, she couldn't find any downside to staying at the McCormack estate. The only negative she could see was having to give up living in the lap of luxury after six months.

Stalling for a few more moments, she asked, "Any particular reason? Besides the fact that my apartment would give you a serious case of claustrophobia after living in a place bigger than most third-world countries."

"There's plenty of room for you and the children. And it's a McCormack tradition to live at the family homestead." He smiled, but it wasn't his usual relaxed grin. "Besides, I think the isolation will be beneficial. Because of the custody hearing," he added quickly.

She couldn't figure out what difference it would make, and wondered at his use of the word "isolation." But he'd conceded every one of her points. It was imperative they look like a happily married couple. With servants and his family there, she wouldn't be *alone* with him. All things considered, it seemed like a win for her and the children. She didn't see any need to fight it.

"All right."

"What do you say to an evening wedding? Day after tomorrow?" he asked. "My legal team can rush the paperwork and I'll have some of the estate staff help pack you and the kids."

It felt quick. Because it was, she thought ruefully. But

he'd said the sooner the better. And his reasoning was eminently sound.

"All right," she said again.

Her stomach dropped as if she'd jumped out of a sky-diving plane for the first time. But this wasn't her first marriage and that was the bad news. Because of *numero uno,* she hadn't ever wanted to take the wedlock walk again.

Her head spun. How had this happened? Forty-eight hours ago she'd spilled coffee on him and vowed to find a way to clear the Hewitt name. Now she was marrying the guy and *changing* her name to McCormack. In the contrition department, that seemed excessive. When apprehension threatened to pull her under, she reminded herself that it was to their mutual advantage.

She almost believed that. This deal was mostly for her, but she was desperate. Somehow she would make it up to him. But she was going into *this* marriage with her eyes wide open. On her terms. She was in control. Yesiree.

But when Quentin turned the full power of his blue eyes on her, she couldn't help thinking that control was such a tenuous thing.

Quentin stood in the great room of his family home. He'd wanted a warm, cozy setting for the wedding and this room with the huge stone fireplace was just right. His mother had risen to the decorating challenge on very short notice. It looked perfect. And this is where he and Dana would face the justice of the peace in just a little while to become man and wife.

His heart beat faster at the thought and he had to remind himself that, while the setting was flawless, everything between him and Dana was far from it.

"So what do you think?" Amanda McCormack asked.

At the sound of his mother's voice, Quentin turned to see her standing on the thick carpet in the foyer.

"I didn't hear you, Mom," he said, straightening his already perfect silk tie. "Thanks for everything you did for tonight. This room looks amazing."

"You're very welcome."

Nothing in her softly lined, still attractive face gave a clue to what she thought. Her blue eyes, so like his, gazed serenely at him. She was a small woman, about Dana's height. Amanda would see eye-to-eye with Dana, literally, he told himself. Her brown hair was carefully colored to hide the sprinkling of gray, and arranged in a simple, smooth gently turned-under style that suited her. In her royal-blue knit dress with its high neckline and long sleeves, she was the picture of elegance and sophistication. But Quentin knew she never forgot that she'd been a struggling single mom when she fell in love with his stepfather. Another reason he knew she would see eye-to-eye with his bride-to-be.

Dana. A warm feeling stole over him knowing that she and the triplets were already upstairs getting ready for the ceremony. It had pleased him that the first meeting between her and his folks had gone well. He had broken the news to his mother and stepfather that he was getting married, then he'd asked for their help in readying the house for the wedding while he took care of the other details. He was grateful that they'd respected his decision and not demanded explanations. But he had a feeling his reprieve was over.

"Tell me again how you and Dana met."

"I haven't told you anything yet, Mom. For Pete's sake, I'm not a teenager. You don't have to use conversational subterfuge to worm stuff out of me,'' he said, trying to deflect her.

''Why is that, dear?'' she asked. ''That you didn't say anything to us about Dana?''

''No particular reason,'' he answered casually. ''Maybe I didn't want to get your hopes up.''

''Have I been that transparent?''

He laughed. ''There's nothing to see through. You come right out and say what's on your mind. Do the words 'Get off your duff, find me a daughter-in-law. I'd like some grandchildren before I'm too old to enjoy them' sound familiar?''

''It's a mother's job to guide her children,'' she said evenly. But her eyes twinkled.

''I'm too old for guidance, Mom.''

''No you're not, dear. So, tell me about this woman who bagged Storkville's most eligible bachelor.''

''Bagged?'' he asked, raising one eyebrow. ''You make me sound like the prize catch at a coon hunt.''

Ignoring his sarcasm, his mother continued. ''How did you meet? *When* did you meet? At what moment did you know she was the one? Why haven't we heard about her before?'' She took a breath, then said, ''Give, Quentin. Details. On the double.''

''Amanda, my dear, cut the boy some slack.'' Carter McCormack joined them and slipped an arm around his wife's small waist.

He was a handsome, silver-haired man, debonair in his dark suit, gray silk shirt and matching tie. His tall physique showed his efforts to stay in shape. Quentin had been barely a teenager when the man came into their lives. But he remembered clearly how Carter had swept his mother off her feet. Ever since, he'd been the father Quentin had always wanted. He loved him.

They had wanted more children, but it hadn't happened. Carter had said Quentin was his son in every way but biological and had made him heir to the family fortune.

"Hi, Dad. Thanks for running interference. Don't think I don't appreciate it. But I really want to tell you about Dana. Both of you."

Now with divine intervention, he would come up with the right words so that they wouldn't question his sanity.

"We met at the ribbon-cutting ceremony for the day-care center." That much was the truth.

His mother tapped her lip and frowned as she thought. "Isn't that when you came home early to change your pants because a child had spilled on you? And your trousers were so stiff you couldn't sit down with your best friend, Mr. Computer?"

"Yeah." He ignored her sarcasm, surprised that she remembered the day. Although meeting Dana had made it memorable for him.

"Lukas did it? That sweet boy I met upstairs?"

He smiled. "Lukie is something else."

"As are those two little girls. Too sweet for words. All three of Dana's children are completely adorable," Amanda said. "And not difficult to see why. Their mother is—what's the right word now? Hot."

"Mom!"

"Don't pretend to be shocked, dear. You've known me for a long time. Now I want to know more about Dana."

"Okay. She's the manager of Bassinets and Booties in town. She moved here with the children about six months ago, after her husband died," he added.

No point in telling them that she was still in love with the man. That would make Amanda worry. Years ago, when it was just him and his mom, he'd gotten in the habit of protecting her. Old habits died hard.

She shook her head. "So all this time we thought you were at the office working late every night, you were actually falling in love with Dana," his mother pronounced.

"It's a comfort to know that some things don't change," he said lightly. "You're still jumping to conclusions, aren't you, Mom?"

"It's not a big leap," his mother retorted. "After all, you're marrying her. But, isn't it a bit fast?" she asked, her maternal concern showing.

Quentin shrugged, he hoped casually. "Dana and I agreed that there's no reason to wait. Besides, time's wasting if we're going to file a joint tax return next year."

"Be still my heart." His mother playfully fanned herself with her hand. In a feigned southern accent, she said, "You fairly turn a girl's head with your romantic notions."

"I cannot tell a lie."

Or worry her with the suspicions of him being the abandoned twins' father. The stability of a family would cement his reputation, and possibly offset a worst-case scenario. If it were just him, he wouldn't care. But stock prices could plummet. Investors could lose a lot of money. Some of them counted on it for retirement, college funds for children. He would do his best to keep that from happening.

And for a long time now, his mother had been after her only son to settle down. Quentin knew she was happy for him, and he refused to spoil this night for her by explaining that it was temporary. Until his DNA test results were in, he wanted his mother in the dark about the evidence against him. Not just to spare her.

The less people who knew, the better his chances of keeping it from Dana. He didn't want her to have any questions about the man she was marrying. He was relieved that he'd gotten this far without her finding out about that damn heirloom rattle found with the twins. If he ever discovered who had taken it…

He couldn't go there. In a short time Dana would be his wife and, with a little luck, he would have the proof of his innocence before they even had to discuss the matter.

Carter hugged his own wife closer to his side. "What your mother means is it's our wish that you and Dana will be as happy as we've been, son."

"Thanks, Dad."

Amanda moved in front of Quentin, stood on tiptoe and kissed his cheek, then followed up with a big hug. "That goes for me too, sweetheart. I don't have the words to tell you how very happy I am," she said.

Just then a black-uniformed maid entered. "Sir, madam, Judge Claybourne has arrived. He's waiting in the parlor."

"Thank you, Jane. Carter, let's go meet with him."

"All right, my dear."

Just after they left, Quentin heard children's voices. He moved into the foyer and saw Dana and the triplets just as they stepped off the last stair. The vision she made stole all the breath from his lungs and he couldn't find the will to care.

Her cream-colored satin dress was sleeveless and scoop-necked. More important, it molded to every luscious feminine curve. Demure matching gloves covered her hands and arms to just above her wrists. A chiffon scarf dangled from her bent elbows. Mahogany curls sat precariously on the crown of her head while stray locks teased her heart-shaped face and the nape of her neck.

How he wanted to press his lips to the exposed skin there and see if she was really as soft as she looked. His mother was right. *Hot* was definitely the appropriate trendy term to describe her. And just looking at her— his body temperature climbed to the danger point.

Lukas ran over to him and wrapped both arms around one leg. "Hi, Mr. Mac. Mommy pretty," he said pointing to his mother.

"Hi, Lukie." Quentin cleared his throat as he absently rubbed the boy's shoulder. "Pretty? That's an understatement. Mommy stunning," he said hoarsely.

"Thank you," Dana answered, her shy smile an indication that she wasn't accustomed to compliments.

He glanced at the girls, who were wearing identical green velvet dresses. With their hair, the same color as their mother's, pulled back from their faces and secured by a matching three-dimensional bow, they were heartbreakers-in-training. Lukas wore navy blue slacks and a white shirt with a red bow tie at his throat. Crooked, but still there. His brown hair was slicked down for the moment, but there was a good chance the prince of perpetual motion couldn't keep it that way for long.

"The triplets look great, too." He met Dana's gaze and didn't miss her smile at his compliment to the kids. Or that it was followed swiftly by a frown of apprehension. Uh-oh. Was she getting cold feet? "Ready?" he asked.

"Honestly? No."

Chapter Five

Dana had never been less ready in her life. The first time she'd said vows, she'd been deeply entrenched in the adoration stage of her relationship. She'd been too naive to know what she was getting into. But she was older now, and jaded. Whoever had coined the phrase "older and wiser," as if it was a good thing, hadn't walked in her wedding shoes the first time down the aisle. Now she knew enough to be very, very afraid.

What if she was making an even bigger mistake than she had with her first marriage? At least then she'd been in love. Now she felt like a corporate acquisition.

"When am I marryin' you?" Lukas asked Quentin.

Molly and Kelly shyly walked over to him and looked up. "We want to get married, too," Molly said.

"As soon as your mom says the word," he answered.

The smile he bestowed on her children and his wonderful way with them multiplied her anxiety by a hundred. She was afraid of making another mistake. She didn't want to be hurt again. Or let them be hurt. Instinct told her that if she dropped her guard for a moment, Quentin was just the man who could tenderize her hardened heart, then grill it into ashes.

He looked so handsome, her heart thumped painfully in her chest. In his dark suit and off-white shirt with matching satin tie, he could have been a male model. A boutonniere of baby's breath and a single white rose graced the lapel of his coat, drawing her attention to his impressive chest. The fluttering in the general region of her heart rendered her speechless.

He was, without a doubt, the nicest man she'd ever met. And that scared her. There was a time when she wouldn't have questioned every little thing. She liked his parents. They were genuinely kind people who had embraced her with open arms, unlike her former in-laws. Her children thought Quentin walked on water, for goodness' sake. But what if tomorrow, she woke up and found out he'd changed, that he didn't want anything to do with them—or her? She'd gone through it once. Why should she believe this was different? But the pedestal she'd put Quentin on was getting higher by the minute. If he didn't live up to her expectations, it would be a long drop.

"What's wrong, Dana?" he asked.

"What if we're making a terrible mistake?"

"I don't see how. We agreed that this is the right thing for both of us. And all the safeguards are in place—your prenuptial agreement, and my contract to—" he hesitated, looking at the children as he searched for the right words "—to help you with the kids."

His carefully chosen words, phrasing that wouldn't upset her children, was verbal Prozac for the butterflies bouncing around inside her. That was the second time today that he'd shown her he was thoughtful and thorough. Earlier they had both met with the lawyer and signed papers that spelled out the terms of their arrangement. They were both protected—legally. Emotionally there were no safeguards, but that couldn't be helped. Keeping her children was the most important thing.

She nodded and felt her mouth tremble when she smiled. "Thank you for that, Quentin." She inhaled deeply and said, "Okay. I'm ready now."

"Ya-a-ay," Lukas cried. "We're gonna marry Mr. Mac."

"Hooray," Molly and Kelly said, clapping hands as they jumped in a circle.

"This is certainly a happy group." Amanda McCormack smiled as she walked into the foyer with her husband.

Dana thought again what a handsome couple they were. Her second thought was that they had the biggest home she'd ever seen. When she'd first arrived, she'd joked about leaving a trail of bread crumbs to find her way out. But it was exceptionally lovely and homey in spite of its size.

She'd gotten her bearings somewhat. This was an area removed from the front entrance. They stood in a circular foyer on bone-colored carpet so thick she could have slept like a baby on it. Curved staircases on either side of the room led to the floor above. In the center was a round cherry-wood table covered with an Irish lace doily and a sweet-smelling floral arrangement in an exquisite lead-crystal vase. Beside Quentin's parents stood an older gentleman. He wore a dark suit and conservative tie. His thinning brown hair was artfully arranged over his pate and half glasses rested on the end of his nose.

"Quentin, you remember the judge. Dana, this is Warren Claybourne, a dear friend of Carter's and mine. He's delighted to marry the two of you."

Lukas ran over to the other woman and said, "We're gonna marry Mr. Mac, too."

"I know, sweetheart," she said, stooping down to his level as she took his hands and gently squeezed them. "And I couldn't be happier. If I were your age, I would be jumping up and down too." She looked at Dana. "You are stunning, my dear."

"Thank you." Dana blushed, remembering that Quentin had said the same thing.

His parents seemed very nice, not to mention delighted that their son was getting married. She couldn't help wondering how he'd explained the speed of this wedding to them. When she met his gaze, he must have seen the question in her eyes, because he nodded slightly, a signal that everything on that score was okay. It was a good thing they weren't alone, or she would have thrown her arms around him and kissed him. Not an especially smart thing to do if she was going to keep her distance.

"Your dress is exquisite," Mrs. McCormack was saying. "It suits you."

"It was my grandmother's," she explained. She hadn't worn it before because Jeff had wanted her in something more befitting the bride of a Hewitt. "I've always loved this dress. It makes me feel like my family is here in spirit."

Carter walked over to her and smiled. "Quentin told us that you have no family to represent you. If you'll let me, I'd be honored to give you away."

"I'd like that very much," she answered, smiling at the handsome older man.

His parents' graciousness made her feel like such a

fraud. If the welfare of her children hadn't been at stake, she would have blurted out the truth. But she and Quentin had agreed to keep the details of the arrangement secret. For the sake of the impending custody battle, everyone must believe that this was a real marriage and they were in love.

Again Quentin must have read her thoughts, because he stepped to her other side and slipped his arm around her waist as if they were a *real* couple who truly adored each other. When she looked into his eyes a thrill shot through her at the expression of appreciation there.

Her heart fluttered like hummingbird wings. If the man had a flaw, she couldn't see it. But then skepticism reared its ugly head. Don't go there, she thought. Not now. For the time being, she would savor the secure feeling of standing between two strong men who seemed to want to protect her.

The judge cleared his throat. "Are you ready to begin? Where do you want me?"

Quentin held out his hand indicating the great room. "In here, sir."

"I'll show you, Warren," Mrs. McCormack said, leading the way. "Places, everyone. Quentin, you come too," she said, taking charge. "Carter, you and Dana stay here until we're set up. Lukas, Kelly, Molly, come along with me."

"I almost forgot." Quentin walked back into the foyer and picked up a bouquet of greenery, baby's breath and white roses. It had been hidden from her view by the impressive arrangement on the table. "This is for you."

"It's so beautiful," she said, taking it from him. Perfume from the flowers wafted to her. As she gazed at him, his image began to waver through the moisture in her eyes. As busy as he'd been arranging everything, he still had time to think about a bride's bouquet. His thoughtfulness was too much. "I didn't even think about flowers to carry. Thank you."

"You're welcome."

"Quentin, dear," his mother said. "The children are being absolute angels. But they have a very small supply of patience. I strongly suggest you get this ceremony under way as soon as possible."

"Let's have a wedding," he said, then turned and walked across the foyer into the great room.

Dana and her father-in-law-to-be waited for their cue. For the first time she was able to study the room off the foyer through the large, square opening. It was so lovely she almost forgot to breathe. The lofty ceiling was highlighted by decorative white crown molding that enhanced the simplicity of the light gray walls.

There were fresh flowers everywhere, including large bouquets on either side of the huge stone fireplace, where a cozy blaze flickered. On the mantel rested a three-dimensional spray of flowers with white candles on either end. The setting was a fairy tale come to life.

The judge stood in front of the fire with Quentin to his left. The triplets stood next to him, then Mrs. McCormack, who watched expectantly. "You're on," she said.

Carter extended his arm. "If you're ready?"

"No guts, no glory," she said, placing her trembling fingers in the crook of his elbow.

He covered her gloved, shaking hand with his own and smiled as he squeezed reassuringly. "Not to worry, my dear. My wife was right. You're definitely *hot.*"

Her jaw dropped as her gaze snapped up to meet his. She saw the twinkle in his brown eyes. "Mrs. McCormack said that?"

"Scout's honor," he answered, holding up three fingers.

She couldn't help laughing, and the humor relaxed her tension. She knew that had been his intention and was terribly grateful to him. At that moment, he led her into the other room and stopped in front of the judge.

"Who gives this woman to be married to this man?" he asked.

Carter kissed her cheek and said, "My wife and I do."

"Me, too," Lukas piped up.

"And me," Molly and Kelly said.

"I think it's unanimous." Quentin laughed as he took her hand in his own.

Dana's stomach quivered at his touch and her chest felt tight, as if she would never take another deep breath. He slipped his fingers into hers and together they faced the judge.

With the book open in front of him he said, "Is there anyone present who knows of any reason why these two should not be joined in holy wedlock?"

Dana thought Quentin tensed for a moment, but figured it was just her own anxiety coupled with an overactive imagination.

"Is it really necessary to ask that?" he asked, an edge to his voice.

He must be more nervous than she'd thought.

The judge smiled. "Habit, my boy. Now, do you want the short or long version of the ceremony?" he asked.

Dana met Quentin's gaze and together they said, "Short."

Judge Claybourne nodded. "Do you, Quentin, take this woman to be your lawfully wedded wife? To have and to hold, in sickness and in health, to love and cherish till death do you part?"

"I do," he answered in a clear, deep voice.

When she was asked the same thing, Dana said, "I do."

"Are you exchanging rings?"

"No," Dana said.

"Yes," Quentin answered at the same time.

Shocked, she glanced at him, then watched Mr. McCormack reach into his pocket and place two gold bands, one with inset diamonds, on the book. She couldn't believe he'd remembered that detail. A loving, committed couple would exchange rings. She shook her head slightly as she sent Quentin a grateful look.

The judge cleared his throat to get her attention. Then he looked over his spectacles and said, "Dana, you might want to have Amanda hold your bouquet for this part."

She handed her flowers and gloves to Mrs. McCormack. When the ring slid on her finger, several things raced through her mind. A—this was really happening. She was *really* getting married. And B—how in the world had he known the size of her finger? The ring fit as if it had been made for her.

When that part of the ceremony was over, they stood facing each other, holding hands. Apparently she was the only one with concerns, because Quentin looked enormously pleased.

The judge cleared his throat. "May I present to you, Quentin and Dana McCormack. You may kiss your bride, my boy."

Intensity darkened Quentin's eyes and Dana somehow knew it was all focused on her. And what a heady feeling it was to have his undivided attention. He slipped one arm around her waist and gently pulled her to him. With his other hand cupping her cheek, he slowly lowered his head. Dana held her breath—waiting, anticipating. The meeting of their mouths was warm and wonderful, sweet and soft. But it was the promise there that sent her pulse pounding to the uh-oh point. The kiss seemed a pledge of what could be—if she would let it.

He tightened his hold, snuggling her more securely against him as he deepened the contact. Dana slipped her arms around his strong neck, sliding her fingers into the soft hair at his nape. Heart pounding painfully in her chest, she opened her mouth when he traced it with his tongue. With their bodies so close, she felt his breathing quicken with her acceptance. He hunched his shoulders forward, surrounding her as he settled in for a thorough exploration of her mouth. Then Dana felt a tugging on her dress.

"Mommy?"

Dazed, she looked down at her son and blinked to bring him into focus. She was very glad that Quentin's arms still held her, steadying her. "Lukie?" she said, breathless.

"Are we married yet?" her son asked.

The words dissipated her sensual haze like a shot of adrenaline. She lowered her arms, and sighed regretfully when Quentin did the same. "Yes, sweetie. We're married."

"Ya-a-ay," he said.

Mrs. McCormack moved beside them. "Congratulations," she said, hugging Dana. Then she stood on tiptoe and kissed her son's cheek before embracing him. "Much happiness, sweetheart."

"Thanks, Mom."

"There's a buffet supper set out in the dining room," she said.

Dana was overwhelmed by their generosity—and her

own guilt. "You shouldn't have gone to so much trouble. We just wanted a small ceremony. Mrs. McCormack—"

"Right back at ya'," the woman said.

"Excuse me?" Dana blinked.

"You're Mrs. McCormack now, too," the woman pointed out.

"That's right," Dana answered, trying to smile.

If only this were the happy, traditional occasion they believed, instead of the act of desperation it truly was.

Quentin watched with supreme male appreciation the sight of Dana backing out of the triplets' room. She'd changed out of her wedding attire into a long-sleeved gray T-shirt and worn black knit pants that caressed her shapely derriere like a lover's hand. A sense of contentment settled over him. A feeling that finally his life had meaning, and was somehow complete. But that didn't take the edge off his need. It only made him want her more.

She took a last loving, protective look at her children, then left the door ajar before turning away. She spotted him in the large sitting area separating that bedroom from the master and bath in this particular suite. There was a floral couch and matching love seat in shades of cream, hunter green and coral. Oak occasional tables were arranged around the furniture, and a TV tucked into a corner entertainment center completed the area. He hoped she liked it—but not so much that she couldn't be persuaded to share his suite, just next door. When she was ready.

"I don't believe you," she said.

Oh, Lord. He hadn't said that out loud, had he? But

she was smiling, so he figured she was referring to something besides his lust.

"What?" he asked.

"With everything you had to take care of, how in the world did you manage it?"

"What everything? And define it."

"The flowers, my bouquet, the food, the rings." She stopped for breath. "And three twin beds for my children. Don't even try to tell me they were already in that room. I saw the marks in the carpet. There used to be a queen-sized bed in there—minimum. And you did it all in such a short time."

"Mom helped. And I can dial a phone and delegate," he said with a shrug. "No big deal."

"It's a very big deal."

He shook his head. "Not even in the same league with you."

"What are you talking about?"

He glanced at the door behind which three three-year-olds were peacefully sleeping. "Don't even try to tell me getting them bedded down is nothing." He tapped his chest. "I was there."

"And you're wearing the evidence to prove it." She glanced at the wet marks bathtime had left on his jeans. Lukas had dumped a glass of water over his head, and Quentin, in an attempt to rinse the soap from his hair. By himself. She smiled. "Just a word of advice. That raincoat we discussed? Keep it handy."

"I'll remember that." He grinned back. "That was work," he continued. "Bath, drying off, pajamas, hair-combing, teeth-brushing, stories, prayers. And that doesn't count negotiations during a sit-down strike—in triplicate."

"'I am woman, hear me roar,'" she said breezily.

"Besides, you carried up two of them. I only had to take one. That cut down negotiating time by a third."

"Don't be so modest. Every night must be a major undertaking, the likes of which hasn't been seen since the invasion of Normandy on D day."

"You're exaggerating."

"Only a little. Seriously, Dana. How do you manage it without your husband? You must miss him in—a lot of ways."

He could have kicked himself when the warm laughter in her eyes was replaced by an emotion he couldn't quite place. It could have been anger and hurt, or abject sadness. He wished he'd kept his mouth shut, because now he'd given her an opportunity to talk about how much she yearned for the love she'd lost. The longer he knew her, the more he wanted to be the only man in her life. He didn't want to share her with the memory of another man.

"Actually I got used to handling the triplets by myself. He was busy," she said vaguely.

Her expression shut him out as surely as if she'd lowered the blinds in her front window. He sensed there was more to it than that, but it was probably too painful for her to talk about. Would she ever get over her boundless love for the husband she'd lost? Enough to let someone else into her heart?

He cautioned himself to take things slow—one step at a time. They were married. He breathed a sigh of relief for that fact. With the suspicion of paternity hanging over his head, he'd been afraid something would upset his plans. That hadn't happened. Now he wanted to establish a trusting relationship with Dana. The last thing their fragile, budding bond needed was for her to hear about the ugly allegations concerning him.

He swore silently. If only he didn't have to wait for DNA results. If only he could tell Dana what was going on and trust her to understand. He longed for a partner, a woman he could share everything with, the wife who would trust him completely in spite of evidence to the contrary. He longed for the time that he could explain to her everything at the same time he could prove his innocence. If there was any justice, it would happen that way.

In the meantime, he hoped the sheriff kept his word to conduct the investigation discreetly. He didn't want Dana upset. He hoped she would never have a single reason to question her trust in him. And as much as he didn't want to know how much she'd loved her husband, he sensed that she needed to talk about it. If she was going to get over her terrible loss, sharing the burden was the first step. Then maybe she could put it in the past and move on.

"You're the one who pulled off a major accomplishment today," she said. "It's no exaggeration to say that the wedding went off without a hitch."

"Just one," he countered. "You and me. We're hitched."

"Cute, Quentin," she teased. "But really, I can't believe how wonderful your parents are. They couldn't have been nicer to me and the children. In spite of the fact that they must have been pretty surprised when you told them."

"Some."

"Some? That's diplomatic."

He watched her tuck a curl behind her ear and suppressed the almost overwhelming urge to press his lips to the soft skin she had just revealed. She was standing right in front of him. Without moving, he could reach out and pull her into his arms. And he wanted to, almost more than he wanted to take his next breath. But he sensed that she would have to set their pace. Assuming they had a pace to set.

"Mostly they're relieved that I'm finally settling down," he added.

"Would you have backed out if you'd known what an undertaking it is to settle down the triplets?"

"No." Who knew one word, a negative, could light her face like a ray of sunshine after a storm? That single syllable dispelled her serious look and she smiled sweetly.

"Right answer," she quipped. Then she moved closer, stood on tiptoe and kissed his cheek. She quickly stepped back and said, "You don't have to help, you know."

His cheek was warm from her kiss and the heat was spreading. Every instinct urged him to take her in his arms, and with every intention of *not* kissing her cheek. He longed to continue the exploration of her mouth that he'd begun after saying "I do."

"On the contrary," he said, then cleared his throat. "I enjoyed it." Especially her thank-you. "And I venture to say you wouldn't turn down an extra pair of hands," he said, holding his own up.

"It would be stupid to turn down an offer like that," she answered. Under her breath she added, "Very nice hands."

Quentin saw her shiver. He knew he wasn't meant to hear the words, but he had. He wanted to show her what those words uttered in that husky, seductive whisper did to him.

As he met her gaze, her eyes darkened from light gray to pewter. And he saw apprehension, even as he noticed that the pulse point in her neck fluttered wildly. Did she feel something for him too?

He wanted to find out. He couldn't have been that wrong about her response to their traditional wedding ceremony kiss. And it had been in front of her children and virtual strangers. She'd forgotten all of that and kissed him back. Big time. And a minute ago, she had bussed his cheek—voluntarily. He took a step toward her.

"Dana, I—"

She crossed her arms over her chest and walked past him, as far away as she could get and still stay in the same room. "Quentin, I want to thank you for something else," she said, a tremor in her voice.

"What's that?"

"Separate bedrooms."

"Right," he said, running a shaking hand through his hair.

"This suite is lovely and I'm grateful to you for making us feel so at home. But I—I'm wondering about that connecting door?"

He watched her stand up a little straighter, as if she was bracing herself for the worst. "We agreed to pose as a couple in love."

"I remember."

"It's hard to do that in separate bedrooms. And servants gossip. So I chose this suite for you and the children because of the connecting door."

"Oh." She touched a hand to her mouth. "What if I leave some of my clothes scattered around your room?"

"Okay. And I'll take care of the rest of the evidence."

A becoming flush stained her cheeks. She knew he meant twisted sheets. "You really did think of everything. Nine out of ten men would push for their husbandly rights. I appreciate your sticking to the letter of our agreement.''

Her reminder was about as subtle as a high-pitched whistle. Sleeping in separate bedrooms was the only part of that agreement he'd wanted to dig his heels in and fight. It frustrated him that she'd taken away his ability to give her the one thing she didn't already have—intimacy with a man, closeness as a couple. Something that he was more and more beginning to see that he wanted.

But now wasn't the time to push. He sensed that they could have something—given the time and luck it needed to grow.

She wasn't ready to pick up the pace of their relationship. He would give her a little more time before *he* did.

Chapter Six

A week after the wedding Dana ushered the triplets into the imposing house through the back entrance that led to the kitchen. She'd discovered soon enough that it was cleaner that way. She rubbed her hands together trying to speed up her circulation after the cold outside.

"Winter's coming early this year," she said to herself.

It was nice to come home to a place that was warm and safe—even if it *was* temporary. Growing up, she'd felt the kitchen was the heart of the home. It was like that in the McCormack house, too. This room was huge, in proportion with everything else on the estate, but surprisingly homey. Beige tile floor stretched out, interrupted in the middle by an island work center. A refrigerator that seemed as big as her old apartment was on one wall next to a state-of-the-art cooktop, surrounded by hunter-green granite countertops and ample cupboards.

While she'd taken those few moments to appreciate her surroundings, her girls had sat down on the floor.

"Tired, Mommy," Kelly said.

"Me tired too, Mommy," Molly added.

"Wanna see Mr. Mac," Lukas chimed in, running from the room.

Dana hadn't the energy to chase him. She'd worked late—again. Me tired too, she thought, and hungry besides. Unlike her three-year-olds, she couldn't sit down on the floor and announce it. Although her inner child desperately wanted to.

In the seven days since the wedding, they'd settled into a pattern of eating dinner as a family with his folks. She found that the together time was something she looked forward to. When she'd realized today that ordering store merchandise for the Christmas season would take longer than she expected, she'd called to let Amanda know. She'd asked that they not hold up supper for her. And if the spotless, empty kitchen was any indication, they had taken her at her word.

Quentin entered the room holding Lukas, and her son had one arm around his neck. Dana's heart caught at the sight of the two of them. Her son thought Quentin was the best thing since a peanut-butter sandwich with the crust cut off. Her husband walked over to her and kissed her lightly on the mouth, then slipped his arm around her and nestled her to his side. Dana was torn between the spontaneous heat flowing through her, making her want more, and questioning why he'd initiated the intimate *husbandly* gesture.

She had her answer when Amanda and Carter followed on his heels to join them. He was putting on a public show of being a happily married man.

"Hi," Dana said looking up at him, then at his folks. "I'm sorry to be so late. Halloween is two weeks away and that makes Christmas right around the corner. It's my job to make sure we have enough product to sell."

"At least your excuse is better than Quentin's," Amanda said. "Or better than his excuses for working late used to be," she amended. "We never saw him. But since you married my son, he's been home for supper every night."

"Really?" Dana asked glancing up at him. Did his coming home early really have something to do with her? She couldn't stop the glow that started in her center and worked its way outward.

"I've been meaning to tell you about Mom's tragic secret," Quentin said in a stage whisper as one corner of his mouth quirked up. "She exaggerates."

"I do not," his mother countered. "The honest-to-goodness truth is that when you discovered computers, I knew you'd found companionship. But I'll admit I began to worry when you spent so much time at the office. I couldn't help wondering if you were having a ménage à trois with your electronic friend and its acquaintance Ms. Fax."

"And you don't think that's an exaggeration?" Quentin asked her.

Dana laughed at their banter, but the words tugged at her heart because she suspected there was some truth in them. As in: he had worked late all the time. Was Quentin as lonely as she had been? Was he coming home early now just to keep up appearances? Or because he wanted to spend time with her and the children?

Dana looked around the kitchen. "I'm glad you didn't wait dinner for me. Hannah fed the triplets at BabyCare. She's such a mother."

"That's the truth," Amanda said. "She's certainly taken those poor abandoned twins under her wing."

"And how would you know that?" her husband asked.

"I stopped in for a bite at the diner today and Penny Sue Lipton was telling Vern and Doris Feeney that Hannah and Jackson want to take care of Sammy and Steffie permanently."

Carter frowned. "At least whoever walked out on those babies cared enough to leave them with Hannah. But if you ask me, there isn't a place in hell hot enough for the mother and father of those children."

Still holding her, Quentin's arm tensed for a moment and she looked at him. There was an odd, guilty expression on his face that puzzled Dana.

"Hannah certainly loves kids and she managed to combine her calling with her business," she said. "And no one appreciates that more than I do. I was so late, she really went above and beyond the call of duty. Today, I truly don't know what I would have done without her and the day-care center."

"Then it's a good thing Quentin made that generous donation in order to get it up and running." Amanda smiled proudly at her son. She looked at him as if he would sprout wings and straighten his halo any minute.

"Mother," Quentin said, irritation lacing his tone. So much for Saint Quentin.

"You never call me 'Mother' unless you're upset. What gives?" she asked.

No kidding, what gives, Dana thought. Stunned, she looked up at him. "*You're* the mysterious BabyCare benefactor?"

"The operative adjective should be 'anonymous,'" he said, an edge to his voice. "Mother—"

"What?" The older woman looked bemused. "I figured Dana knew."

"No one was supposed to know. Which makes me wonder—how did you find out?"

"We share an accountant, dear."

"Whatever happened to confidentiality?"

"I'm your mother. There's no such thing as maternal confidentiality."

"There should be," he muttered.

There was a tone to his words and a pinched, angry look around his mouth that seemed out of proportion.

"For Pete's sake, Quentin, the way you're acting it's as if you're hiding something." Amanda put her hands on her hips as she frowned at him.

"What would I be hiding?"

The question was meant to be rhetorical, but his manner was nowhere near as relaxed as usual, making Dana wonder why.

"It was a good deed," she said. "You're my hero."

"If the media gets hold of this, who knows what they'll concoct. Facts can be manipulated to create a false impression," he said. "Besides, I wanted it kept quiet because I didn't want any fanfare."

"We can keep a secret." Carter shook his head. "Don't worry, son. There's not a fan in sight. As for fare—" he looked at Dana "—we're planning to take you and Quentin and the children out to dinner."

"That's very nice of you," she said gratefully. "But I wish you'd gone ahead. Like I said, the children have already eaten. And it's so late. As you can see from their sit-down strike, they need to be in bed. And I still have to give them baths. After that I'll just have a sandwich."

"Mom and Dad, you go ahead," Quentin said. "I'll help Dana, then make sure she eats."

"If you're certain?" Amanda said doubtfully.

Quentin put Lukas down then stepped between his

parents and slipped his arms through theirs as he escorted them to the door. "You two crazy kids have a good time. Don't come home past curfew and don't get into any trouble," he said.

"Don't take that tone with me, young man," his mother joked. "You're not too big to put across my knee."

Dana laughed at the idea of the petite woman disciplining her strapping son. "You guys have a nice dinner. Dress warm, it's cold out there. Aunt Gertie says that winter is coming early this year."

"Yeah," Quentin said wryly. "We should all put our trust in a woman who swears her lemonade causes pregnancy."

"Don't listen to him," Dana scoffed. "And don't worry. I'll keep him in line."

"Thank you, dear. You're just the woman who can do it," Amanda said just before Quentin closed the door behind them.

Dana wanted to tell her she was wrong about that. She hadn't been able to keep Jeff in line, and she'd come to find out that love was a mirage. But she didn't even have love leverage with Quentin, not even the illusion of it. They had a business arrangement, nothing more. No matter how much the last seven days made her wish that it could be different.

Every night since they married, he'd played dolls with the girls, roughhoused with Lukie, turned his hands into wrinkled-up prunes helping with baths, and read Dr. Seuss until he swore he did not like green eggs and ham. But she sure as shootin' liked him. He'd been completely wonderful.

She'd begun to wonder if he really did want to settle down, as his mother had said. Maybe his proposal wasn't so sudden as it had seemed. Did he want something more? Something deeper with *her?* Could this solicitous Quentin be real, and could it last?

If her past history was anything to go by, the answer was no.

Not long after his folks had left, Quentin watched Dana kiss the kids good-night, the same way he had every night since their wedding. He liked being part of the routine more and more each time and knew this was what he'd been searching for, waiting for. The downside was that he also realized that it could disappear in the blink of an eye.

Dana now knew he was the mysterious day-care benefactor. Who could have known that his simple desire to avoid publicity would make him look guilty of something? He reminded himself that it was a single piece of information. She didn't know about the McCormack heirloom rattle found with the babies. Only together did those two pieces begin to build a puzzle that made him look bad.

Again he wondered how long before the DNA results would be back. If Dana found out before… He refused to go there.

She stopped beside him in the doorway and he resisted the urge to slip his arm around her waist. That wasn't the way to win his wife and favorably influence her affections.

"Good night, kidlets," she said.

"'Night, Mommy. 'Night, Mr. Mac." Lukas blew him a kiss.

Quentin had learned early on that these three could drag out bedtime ad infinitum. He'd figured out that blowing kisses from the doorway was the best graceful exit he could hope for

"Good night, Lukie, Molly, Kelly." He blew an imaginary kiss from the palm of his hand to each of them.

"Mommy?"

"Yes, Molly?"

How did Dana know which of the girls had spoken? Quentin wondered. It was too dark in here to see the beauty mark.

"Why don't you kiss Mr. Mac good-night?"

Surprised, Dana glanced nervously at him, then back at her daughter. "Because we're not going to bed yet."

"Oh."

It was quiet for a moment, but Quentin could almost hear wheels turning in their creative, three-year-old minds. He wasn't disappointed.

"Mr. Mac, when it's grown-up bedtime, are you gonna kiss her then?" Lukas asked.

He looked at Dana. He *wanted* to. Every night, alone in bed, he'd thought about nothing else. Nothing except having her next to him, warming his bed, his blood, his heart. And kissing her and taking her with him to the next level and the release that waited for both of them. Where Dana was concerned, blowing kisses just wouldn't cut it.

But she had given him no sign that she was ready to pick up the pace of their relationship.

Dana answered for him. "Enough questions. It's past time for you guys to go to sleep."

Together, they backed out of the room and she left the door ajar. Quentin looked down at her and noticed the weariness in her gray eyes, the tense set of her shoulders.

"You haven't eaten yet, missy," he scolded.

"I'm not sure which is more important—food or sleep." She sighed. "Since I'm too tired for food, I guess I'll go with getting some shut-eye."

He noticed that she avoided using the word "bed." "You come right over here," he said, taking her elbow to lead her to the couch. With his hands on her shoulders, he gently urged her onto the soft cushions. Then he lifted her legs and rested them on the coffee table.

"Don't move until I get back," he ordered.

As her eyes drifted closed, she said, "It's a good thing for you that I'm too tired to argue." One eye opened. "And don't call me missy."

"Yes, ma'am." Grinning, he saluted before leaving her.

Quentin went to the kitchen. Not wanting to disturb the cook this late, he rooted through the refrigerator. There was leftover pot roast, mashed potatoes and green beans from supper the night before. While it was heating in the microwave, he pulled out a tray and assembled silverware, napkin, wine and two glasses on it. He wished he had a red rose, but he was winging this.

When everything was ready, he carried the tray upstairs and found Dana exactly where he'd left her.

"Supper is served," he said softly and watched her eyelids flutter open.

Did she have any idea how innately sexy that movement was? Or how much he wanted to see it beside him first thing every morning? He pushed away the thought. No way would he take advantage of an overworked mother of triplets, no matter how much he wanted her.

She pushed herself up and put her feet on the floor while he set the tray on the coffee table in front of her.

She began to eat. "I didn't realize how hungry I was

until I smelled this,'' she said popping another bite of potatoes into her mouth.

He poured wine into two long-stemmed crystal glasses and set one on her tray. ''I hate to be a walking, talking cliché, but you really do need to eat, to keep your strength up. The mother of three can't afford to get run-down.''

''Especially if she wants to maintain custody of said three.'' She frowned.

''My lawyers are working on the case. Have you heard any more from the Hewitts?'' he asked sharply.

She shook her head. ''But...''

He sat down beside her. Since she was in the middle of the sofa, he had no choice but to sit close, with their thighs brushing. Although she tried to hide it, he didn't miss her small intake of breath at the contact. Or the quick sip of wine she swallowed.

''What?'' he coaxed.

She sighed as she put her fork down and set the napkin beside her plate. Still holding her wine, she sat back on the couch, angling toward him with her feet curled to the side.

''There are way too many days like today,'' she said.

''Define 'a day like today.'''

''Long.''

''Embellish, please. You strike me as the conscientious type who isn't afraid of long days and hard work.''

''Yeah, I'm a real pioneer woman. Salt of the earth, stiff upper lip and all that,'' she said smiling a sad, tired smile that went straight as an arrow to his heart.

''All joking aside, Dana, tell me what's got you down. It might help to talk about it.'' And set a pattern of trust and confidence.

She sent him a skeptical look. ''Okay, here goes. The

kids are in day care practically from sunup till way after sundown. When we get home, dinner is rushed because they need to get to bed. Because if they don't get enough sleep, the next day is a nightmare. Bedtime routine is important, starting with baths.'' She flashed him a wry look. ''You've been baptized every night. You know about that.''

''Yeah,'' he said, glancing at the spots on his jeans that were almost dry now. ''It's my favorite part.''

''Thank goodness for Hannah, or I would have had to feed them tonight. At least we got to play a little longer because of her.'' She stared pensively into the golden liquid in the glass she twirled between her fingers. ''Sometimes I think they might be better off with the Hewitts.''

''You don't mean that.''

''At least they would have carefree quantity time with a couple who loves them.''

''What are we? Chopped liver?'' he asked. He was masquerading as their father, but it wasn't an act. Every day he cared about those kids more. How could he not? They were delightful. ''You're their mother. No one could love them more or give them quality time like you.''

''Time,'' she said, shaking her head sadly. ''A precious commodity. I have so little to go around. My job is demanding. With the holidays just around the corner, it's only going to get worse. The season is for children and should be a happy time, but I'm dreading it.''

Was part of that because it reminded her of the boundless love she'd lost almost a year ago?

No way could he ask her that. Instead he said, ''So quit your job.''

Her gaze snapped up to meet his. ''What?''

The words had popped out, but he found he warmed to the idea. "Why not? Now that we're married, you're not alone. You don't need the money. I have plenty."

"I can't do that."

"It seems like the perfect solution to me. And think about the lawsuit."

"What?" she asked, an edge creeping into her voice.

"It makes good sense. How could the court take the kids away from their mother, a woman who would choose her children over her career?"

"I can't believe you're using my children against me, too."

"What are you talking about? I'm trying to help. And what do you mean *too?*"

"What happens when we separate in six months?" she asked, ignoring his question. "How would I support the children then?"

He'd begun to hope she would forget about that part of the agreement. The raw emotion in her expression said she wasn't even close. "We could cross that bridge when we get there. I could give you—"

"I thought I made it clear that I only want your help to maintain custody of my children. Nothing else, per the prenuptial agreement."

"Believe it or not, Dana, I've come to care a great deal about those children. Damn the prenuptial agreement. Those kids will never want for anything. Ever," he added.

"Just words. Like most men's."

"Most men? So you've known a lot?" he asked, angry that she would lump him with others.

"Not a lot," she admitted. "In fact just one too many."

"And who was he?"

"My husband."

He stared at her. That wasn't the answer he'd expected. "Your husband? But I thought—"

"I knew it couldn't last," she said, shaking her head. She set down her glass and stood up, rounding the coffee table to keep it between them. "I'd begun to think you were different. That your family was different."

"Different how?"

"The Hewitts never liked me. They accused me of being interested in Jeff for his money. But they were wrong. I was in love with him."

Quentin sensed that she was finally going to open up. And somehow he knew he wasn't going to like what she had to say.

"Go on," he encouraged, in spite of his misgivings.

"Over their objections, we got married. Then he changed. It was as if he married me *because* his parents disapproved. I got pregnant right away. He had no tolerance for morning sickness. And even at the beginning, before I needed clothes made by Omar the Tentmaker, he wanted nothing to do with me. He wouldn't touch me or kiss me," she said, before her voice caught.

She was looking down as she wrapped her arms around her waist. Her shoulders drooped and her mouth trembled.

After several moments, she continued. "When three babies were born, he said he hadn't even wanted one, let alone three. That was the first I knew about how he really felt. Before we married he knew how much I wanted children and he agreed. But the demands of triplets cramped his lifestyle. And that's not the worst."

"Tell me," he said, not really wanting to know.

"I found out he was seeing someone else. Maybe more than one someone. Women called the house. I smelled perfume and found lipstick on his clothes.'' She laughed without humor. ''The usual signs. It was as if he wanted me to know.''

Anger churned in his gut. The man had everything and was too stupid to know it. ''What happened?''

''I confronted him and suggested we go to counseling.'' Her whole body tensed. She reached for her wineglass and her hands started shaking so hard, the liquid sloshed dangerously close to the rim. She left it on the table. ''I'd never seen him so angry. He left and I never saw him again. He was killed in a car accident about a mile from the house.''

''Dana, I'm sorry. But—''

''I didn't explain all this for the sympathy vote, Quentin. I just want you to understand that I won't be a victim again.''

She was so strong, he had trouble seeing her as a doormat. Was there more than what she'd already told him?

''He didn't abuse you?'' he asked sharply.

She shook her head. ''Nothing that overt. He isolated me. I had no resources except what he gave me. I had no marketable skills. After he was gone, all I had was a college degree that wasn't worth the paper it was printed on. Without recent work experience I couldn't make enough money to support us. And I was in that fix because I put all my energy into the man I loved and my children.''

''You say it as if it's a bad thing.''

''Only that I was stupid. There was no life insurance. I paid the premium and I saw the statements. The value went down. When I confronted him, he said he was investing it for me and the kids. I believed him. Now I know he spent it impressing other women. I felt manipulated, deceived. He put me right where he wanted me and I let him. Then he was gone and my in-laws refused to help. They'd never changed their opinion of me. I had nowhere to turn."

He shook his head, unable to comprehend anyone treating someone as sweet and wonderful as Dana that way. Not to mention their own grandchildren. "They're obviously selfish, shallow people. But I don't see you as a victim. You pulled your life together pretty fast, lady. Against enormous odds. You found a job here in Storkville and you support your kids without help."

She smiled sadly. "Exactly. And I can't afford to turn my back on that job. I won't be that vulnerable again. I loved him, and he single-handedly and systematically killed my affections."

"I would never do that to you."

"And why should I believe that?"

Quentin was stunned. "Dana, I don't know what to say."

She laughed, but there was no humor in the sound. "Jeff used to *say* all the right things. But everything he *did* was wrong."

A little while ago he thought nothing would make him happier than to hear that she hadn't been in love with her husband. He'd been wrong.

He stood up and moved in front of her. "I'm sorry you had to go through that. But I'm not like Jeff. There's nothing I can do to prove that to you except put one foot in front of the other day after day."

Years ago he'd heard that actions speak louder than words. He never thought he'd have to put it into practice to attain something he badly wanted. But he couldn't think of anything else to do. Holding back was getting him nowhere. It was time to pick up the pace.

Curling his fingers around her upper arms, he gently tugged her to him. "On second thought, there is one thing I can do."

He concentrated on the fluttering pulse at the base of her throat that told him she felt the same way he did. Then he lowered his mouth to hers. He felt her conflict—her hesitation and need. Slowly, he moved his lips over hers, nibbling gently. Her hands, resting at his waist, moved up and over his chest until she looped her wrists around his neck.

Her breasts burned his chest as she molded her curves against the hard planes of his body. She felt more wonderful than he'd imagined. Tiny sounds, soft moans escaped her, encouraging him. His breathing grew labored and he wasn't alone.

"Dana, let me—"

She froze for a moment, then lowered her hands as she drew in a shaky breath. "Quentin, I can't do this."

"Don't tell me you didn't kiss me back."

Her eyes begged him to understand. "That would be a lie. I hate deception. It's way too late to say that I don't find you attractive."

"I hear a *but* coming," he said.

"I won't lead you on. I'm not marriage material any more, thanks to my husband. The only good thing he gave me was the triplets. When my custody of them is secure, you and I will separate. It's always been about business. Would you kiss a business associate, Quentin?"

One corner of his mouth curved up. "Probably not."

"Then please don't complicate our relationship by kissing me again. Let's keep it strictly business." She frowned. "By the way, when do you need me to fulfill my part of our bargain and be of help to you with social functions?''

Social functions were the furthest thing from his mind, but it was one of the arguments he'd used to convince her to marry him.

He let out a long breath. ''There's a costume party here at the estate the Saturday before Halloween.''

''That's two and a half weeks away! When did you plan to tell me?''

''It slipped my mind.'' Along with a lot of other things, since she and the triplets had blown into his life like a tornado. ''I guess I'm not used to having a wife to handle those things.''

''I'll talk to Doleen and your mother and find out what I can do to help.''

He wondered if it occurred to her how odd that they talked about separating one minute, and the next, discussed her role as hostess at the company's Halloween party.

''That sounds good.'' He stared at her full lips. Parties were the last thing he wanted to discuss when he was alone with her. ''But, Dana, about this whole kissing thing—we still have to keep up the appearance of a loving, committed couple—for the custody hearing.''

She hesitated a moment, then insisted, ''We can do that without kissing. I really feel strongly about this. Promise me you won't kiss me again.''

He shook his head. ''I won't lie to you. I can't give you my word on that.''

''At least you're honest.'' She sighed. ''But it's late and I'm tired. I think it's best if we say good night.''

''All right.'' It was best not to push her. He stepped back and ran his fingers through his hair. ''Sleep well, Dana.''

"Fat chance," she said wryly. "But I wish you the same," she whispered as he let himself through their connecting door.

Quentin finally had the big picture, and the only good he could see was that Dana definitely wasn't a gold digger. He'd been looking for a woman who could love him for the man he was, trust him for his character. Someone not just interested in his bank balance. And he was pretty sure he'd found his someone.

But Dana was unlikely to ever believe in anyone again. Especially a man surrounded by suspicions. He knew the DNA results would eventually clear him. But if she ever found out he was a suspect at the time they'd married, she would never believe he hadn't proposed for his own selfish interests. For damage control and the good of company stock prices.

He dragged in a breath. If she ever found out he was suspected of fathering the twins abandoned in the day-care center, he could kiss her goodbye. He smiled humorlessly at the irony. She'd made it clear she didn't intend to kiss him ever again.

But there was still a chance he could change her mind. If the allegations surrounding him remained a secret until he could prove his innocence.

Chapter Seven

"All work and no play—" Quentin raised one eyebrow as he let the statement hang there.

"Makes Dana a dull girl," she finished.

Dana was sitting on the couch in her suite with a blank work schedule for Bassinets and Booties in her lap. It was Saturday and the triplets were playing downstairs with Quentin's folks. He'd just appeared in the open doorway. Had she subconsciously left the door open as an invitation to him?

It had been three days since she'd told him her dark secret, and practically thrown him out when he wouldn't promise not to kiss her again. And he hadn't—promised *or* kissed her. In fact, nothing had changed. He still played with the kids, and gave her a hand at bedtime.

Correction, there was one slight change. He kissed the kids good-night, then left before she finished tucking them in. And always there was a hungry, intense expression on his face that she suspected had a lot to do with wanting to kiss *her*. She probably wouldn't have noticed, except she knew how he felt.

She yearned to kiss him again.

Partly *because* of his behavior. He wouldn't promise not to kiss her and possibly break his word, but he was showing her that he was doing his best to abide by her wishes. A man couldn't be more honorable than that. The thought made her skin hot and turned her insides soft and gooey.

She was so confused. Some people struggled with obsessions about food. She had arguments with herself about Quentin. One minute she planned to be cool and aloof. The next she struggled to keep from going to find him. She flat-out just enjoyed his company. And darn it all, she was glad he'd stopped in to see her now.

"Aren't you supposed to be off on the weekend?" he said, lounging in the doorway. "Is that work you're doing?"

With arms crossed over an impressively wide chest and a mischievous sparkle in his blue eyes, he was definitely a sight for sore eyes. In jeans that were soft and worn in the most interesting places and a white shirt with the sleeves rolled to just below his elbows, he cut quite a masculine figure.

Be still my heart!

"Yes," she agreed. "To both questions."

"Correct me if I'm wrong, but aren't you the store manager? Doesn't rank have its privileges?"

She drew air into her lungs. "Yes to the first question. And to the second: rank has its *responsibilities*. I have to get the schedule done. It's complicated because we have so many part-timers. But the busiest time of year is coming up and I want to make sure the store is adequately staffed, as well as honor any time off requested by the employees."

"Just plug in the holes and let the chips fall where they may," he suggested. "You're the boss."

She slanted a skeptical look at him. "Is that what you would do?"

"Of course," he said too easily. "Being at the top has its perks."

"According to your mother, whom I haven't known long, but have learned to trust implicitly, you have been known to put in an exceptionally long day. So what *do* your employees *do?*" she asked, her voice dripping with sarcasm. "Something tells me you're not the kind of man who lets the chips fall where they may. Or the kind of boss who doesn't care about the needs of the people who work for him."

"I'm wounded that you don't believe me," he said feigning hurt.

"Sell it somewhere else." Nothing she had seen so far could convince her that he would run his business that way.

"Okay, you're right. I subscribe to the simple but effective philosophy that you catch more flies with honey than you do with vinegar. So far, my employees have scored high marks for loyalty."

"I agree with your philosophy. Even as we speak, I'm trying to practice what I preach. Which leaves me with a blank spreadsheet, a honey jar and nowhere to go," she sighed, taking off her glasses.

"Which is why I'm here," he said, smiling the smile that never failed to make her knees go weak and her heart flutter like the wings of a frightened bird.

"You're going to plug up the holes in my schedule with honey?" she asked skeptically.

"No, I'm going to take you away from all this. And I have somewhere to take you away to."

"Oh, really," she said. "And pray tell, where would that be?"

"The pumpkin patch."

She clapped her hands together. "Oh, Quentin, what a wonderful idea." Almost as good as his kiss the other night. Now there was some honey that would catch her. Which was why she had to turn him down. It was dangerous to spend time with him when his charm batteries were one-hundred-percent charged. Like now. Like always.

She looked at the paper in her lap. "But this really needs to be done. And I have laundry, and—"

"I think you're afraid."

"Oh, you do," she said hedging, and hoping he didn't see the heated flush she could feel creeping into her cheeks. If he did, he would know he was right.

"Definitely afraid. And the reason I think that is because you're making excuses."

"What excuses, and what would I have to be afraid of?" Besides another one of his toe-curling kisses. But he couldn't know that.

"My irresistible charm."

So much for him not knowing. "Since it's nonexistent I suppose there's no reason to fear your humility."

"Nope," he said smugly and without shame. "As for your excuses, work would be the first lame one. You're brighter than the average bear. You could whip that schedule out in nothing flat. Laundry would be lame excuse number two. We have a trained staff here to handle that. And just between you and me, they've complained that you're getting in their way and hurting their feelings. They think you do your own laundry because you don't trust them."

"I do it because I'm trying to keep my life real. When custody of the kids is secure, Cinderella goes back to the kitchen."

His frown came and went so quickly, she wasn't sure she'd actually seen it. "An interesting rationalization. But I'm afraid that I must conclude Cinderella is afraid to spend time alone with me."

"There's just one flaw to your theory, Prince Charming." Oh, how perfectly the nickname fit him. "By definition, an outing to the pumpkin patch would probably include the children. Therefore we wouldn't be alone."

"See," he said, as if she'd proven something. "Brighter than the average bear. You don't miss anything. So how about it? Want to go with us?"

"Have you already said something to the triplets?" she asked sharply.

"Do I have stupid written on my forehead? I wouldn't say anything to them without clearing it through you first. But, the weather is brisk and cold, but sunny. And we have to get pumpkins to decorate for the costume party here at the estate. It's just two weeks away. Storkville's new home-and-garden center has Halloween Central set up, with pumpkins galore. It will be fun. And I know someone who hasn't had any fun for a long time."

"You couldn't possibly mean me."

Ignoring her remark, he took a breath, then continued. "And you did ask when your official hostess duties would begin. How about now? You can pick out the official Halloween pumpkin for the official party for my official employees, shareholders and townsfolk. What do you say?"

"That was very persuasive. How could I say no? You're on, hotshot. Let's go tell the children."

She just hoped she didn't regret letting herself be talked into this.

Several hours later, Dana couldn't have been happier that she'd decided to join in the fun. Being with Quentin and her children made her happy. Even when it involved blotting Quentin's pants from the "ritual sliming" as he good-naturedly called it when Lukie inevitably spilled something on him. She couldn't remember the last time she'd felt so carefree or laughed so hard.

Now they stood in the parking area after seeing the children off. Quentin's parents had taken the exhausted three-year-olds home in their car. She and Quentin were going to follow in his.

"Is it written somewhere that at any gathering liquid must be spilled?" he asked.

She knew he was teasing. "You're the adult, Lukie's only three," Dana said defending her son even as she chuckled at the dried red stain on Quentin's jeans. "It's your own fault. This one's on you."

"I'll ignore the pun and go directly to, how is it my fault?"

"Two words—lid and straw."

He nodded, and there was an unmistakable why-didn't-I-think-of-that look on his face. "I guess I have a lot to learn," he admitted.

"Not really. Parenting is two parts common sense and one part iron will. Just say no."

"But Lukie was thirsty. And he wanted punch."

"Then I have no sympathy for you." Dana shivered as the wind blew. "And look on the bright side. With winter coming early, no self-respecting ant would be caught dead outside. You probably won't have to share.''

''Now there's something to celebrate.'' He reached over and wrapped her scarf more tightly around her neck. His knuckles grazed her jaw.

Dana shivered again and it had nothing to do with the chill in the air and everything to do with the magic of his touch. Just a brush of his hand made her tingle from head to toe and kicked up her internal furnace. Definitely magic.

She hadn't thought he could look more appealing than he had lounging in her doorway. She was wrong. He'd added a brown leather bomber jacket and aviator sunglasses to the ensemble. The effect was deadly. She could run, but she was nearly out of places to hide.

''I'm glad Mom and Dad took the kids home,'' he said. ''It's kind of cold out here for them.''

''Yeah. That was really nice of them. I was concerned because the girls are prone to ear infections. And the wind is so cold.''

''Not to mention that they'd had enough.''

''Oh, you think they'd had their fill of pony rides, the haunted house and junk food?'' she demanded playfully. ''Were they weary of having their every wish fulfilled and instantly gratified?''

''Are you saying I'm spoiling them?'' he asked.

''In a word—yes.''

''Okay.'' He nodded thoughtfully as they strolled through the crowd. ''I can accept that. But in my defense, I have to say that it's completely selfish.''

''And how is being selfish a defense?'' she asked.

''When I look at their cute little faces smiling, it makes me smile. I like smiling.'' He shrugged sheepishly. ''Pretty sappy, huh?''

"Pretty nice. Sweet enough to lure those ants from their winter hiding place."

"Now there's an endorsement. Let's go find the perfect party pumpkin, pumpkin."

She narrowed her gaze on him. "Don't ever call me pumpkin, hotshot." He laughed and she put her hand on his arm to halt him. "Maybe we should do this another time. Are you sure Carter and Amanda don't mind taking care of the children?" She studied his face to gauge the sincerity of his answer.

He looked thoughtful. "I can't read their minds, but I do know they parented me. And did a fine job, I might add," he said with a fleeting grin. "They knew what they were getting into. And bottom line, Dana, they volunteered."

At that moment she hated Jeff. She hated that he'd turned her into a cynical shrew who questioned everyone and everything.

"Still." She glanced past the people meandering through the hay bales and pumpkin display in the general direction the kids had gone. "Maybe we should go back and bail out your folks."

"Is that an excuse not to be alone with me?" he asked. "I've been a perfect gentleman," he reminded her.

But the longer they were alone, the less she wanted to be a lady. She knew his remark was left over from their conversation from the other night. It reminded her that there was something she needed to say to him. And with his parents and the children around she hadn't found the right time. Until now.

"Quentin—"

"Dana—"

They looked at each other for a moment before he smiled. "Ladies first."

She took a deep breath, then let it out. "I have to apologize for the other night. You've been kind and generous to me and the triplets. As angry as you must be—"

"Why would I be angry?"

"I practically threw you out of my room. And it's really *your* room. It's just that Jeff Hewitt turned me into a question-everything, trust-no-one kind of person. Because he made a fool of me. I won't let it happen again. I can't afford to. It's my responsibility to protect the kids."

"Except for spoiling them a little, I would never hurt them. Which brings me to why you think if we spend time alone together I'm going to make a fool of you."

She sighed. "At the very least, it wouldn't be hard for me to make a fool of myself. I like you."

"You could have fooled me." One corner of his mouth turned up at his play on words.

"What's not to like? You're charming, intelligent, good-looking and a better-than-average kisser—" She stopped. She couldn't believe she'd said that.

"Just above-average? I was shooting for exceptional. Better than average is a challenge for an overachiever like myself."

He was trying to joke, but this was serious to her. "You promised you wouldn't kiss me again."

"No. You threw me out because I *wouldn't* promise."

"Okay," she said. "But put yourself in my shoes. Jeff swept me off my feet, then lost interest. When someone who looks like you comes at a girl with so much energy—well, after what happened with Jeff I want to run far and fast in the other direction."

"I've been in your shoes, Dana. You know those books about how to marry a millionaire? They practically mention me by name. Women have come on to me with the kilowatts amped up pretty high. When the interest is shallow, it's impossible to sustain the intensity. No woman ever has."

"So you understand where I'm coming from."

"Yes. But what do you say that just for today we forget all that? Stay with me, just long enough to pick out one more pumpkin. After all, didn't Cinderella find a pumpkin that turned into a coach?"

"Yeah, but look what a disaster the ball turned out to be. She lost her shoe, the coach turned back into a pumpkin, and she had to walk home barefoot."

"That was at midnight. And you're throwing up roadblocks. Just say yes. I promise not to kiss you here. After that—I won't lie to you—all bets are off."

He sounded honest. And it would be a baby step in the trust department. After all, even if he broke his word and kissed her senseless, the pumpkins certainly wouldn't mind. And the rest of Storkville? It would be all over town, but definitely a cheap lesson. If he was a wolf in sheep's clothing, wouldn't it be better to know now?

"Okay. Let's do it," she agreed.

He smiled as if she'd just given him the moon. "You're on."

When he held out his arm, and Dana placed her hand in the bend of his elbow, Quentin wanted to shout hallelujah. But how long would the victory last? The kids weren't the only ones who put a smile on his face. Their pretty mother could do it with the slightest touch or a look. But what he wanted to see in her eyes was trust. Unconditional faith in him. Could he be lucky enough to prove his innocence before she even learned of the suspicions?

He'd called the lab, asking when he could expect the results of his DNA test and was told it would be about two more weeks. Maybe less. Mentally, he crossed his fingers and hoped for the latter. For today, he would savor her company.

He enjoyed the occasional brush of their bodies as they moved slowly to the area of the parking lot where pumpkins were displayed on bales of hay under a tarpaulin tent. The sunny weather had brought out quite a few of Storkville's residents, most of whom had heard he and Dana had married. Since they'd arrived, friends and acquaintances had stopped to extend their congratulations. He and Dana had played the happy couple to the hilt. The downside was that all the closeness made it increasingly more difficult to keep his promise not to kiss her in the pumpkin patch. And harder yet to remember that their marriage was only temporary.

Just as they stepped beneath the canvas canopy, there was a flash of light in their faces. When his vision cleared, Quentin saw who had taken the picture. He'd seen her before, covering society soirées and business affairs at the estate. Barbara Kyle, Storkville's social-events reporter.

Of average height, she had curly brown hair and dark eyes. Fresh out of college, she was young and eager. Not to mention ambitious. He'd seen her turn an ordinary function on the estate into the story of the week. She was looking for the scoop that would get her out of the society page and into important news.

"Hi, Quentin," Barbara said. She eyed Dana. "I heard you got married. Are you going to introduce me to your wife?"

"Dana, this is Barbara Kyle, the *Storkville Sentinel*'s society-page reporter. Barbara, Dana Hewitt McCormack, my wife." He found calling her that brought a great deal of satisfaction.

Dana took the hand that the woman held out. "It's a pleasure to meet you."

"Hello. How come you didn't let me cover the wedding?" she asked, looking at him. "It's big-time news when Storkville's answer to Donald Trump gets married."

"Dana and I preferred a small, quiet ceremony just with family."

"Why?"

She was tenacious, he thought. Who, what, when, where, why—the reporter's tools. "Because big and splashy isn't our style. It was for us, not the society page."

"It's still news. People are curious." She eyed him skeptically, then glanced at Dana. "You're the manager of Bassinets and Booties? And you have triplets?"

"Guilty on both counts," Dana answered. "How did you know?"

"I've been asking around. You know the town legend says that the stork who visits Storkville bestows many bouncing bundles on those whose love is boundless."

"That's what I hear," Dana answered, her voice tight.

"The triplets weren't born here," Quentin swiftly interjected.

He wanted to run interference for Dana, protect her from this journalistic barracuda. But he couldn't stifle his satisfaction that she'd confessed that her love for the husband she'd lost wasn't boundless. There was hope for him.

"The wedding was sudden," Barbara said, pointedly

staring at Dana's abdomen. "As far as anyone can tell me, you two didn't know each other before the day-care center's opening."

He felt Dana grip his arm tighter. When he met her gaze, he knew she had something up her sleeve when she looked adoringly up at him.

She batted her eyelashes. "You can't believe how romantic it was with Quentin and me—love at first sight."

He grinned at her. "When it's right, it's right. Why wait?"

"Methinks he doth protest too much." Barbara wagged her finger at him as her brown eyes narrowed. "I smell a story here," she said. "I think there's more to this than meets the eye."

Quentin felt as if there was a boulder the size of Nebraska sitting on his chest. "How can there be more than just the romance?"

"The *Sentinel* dubbed you Storkville's most eligible bachelor. The adjective they left out was *confirmed.* So love at first sight is pretty hard to swallow. Come clean, Quentin. What's really going on?"

She sure had a nose for news. If she kept this up, she would be doing the evening edition in New York before she turned twenty-five.

Quentin met Dana's worried gaze. He knew she was afraid that the custody hearing could be jeopardized if the truth of their relationship was revealed.

Actions spoke louder than words. "I'll show you what's going on."

He pulled Dana against him, bent her back over his arm and pressed his mouth to hers. Distantly, he heard the sounds of laughter, whistles and applause from the people around them. That didn't take the edge off his awareness of her soft lips and sweet sigh. His body responded instantly and he wished they were in the privacy of his room. Completely alone. Reluctantly, he pulled away and saw the dazed, sensuous look in Dana's gray eyes. The good news—he wasn't cold any more.

With an arm around Dana to steady her, he looked at the other woman. "There. That should pretty much explain the situation." Then he took Dana's hand and pulled her with him into the pumpkin patch.

Later he would apologize for breaking his promise. But if it got the bulldog to let loose of her bone, it would be worth it. Secrets were hard to keep in Storkville. It wouldn't take much digging for a determined reporter to learn of the suspicions surrounding him.

Glancing at Dana, he realized he had a lot at stake. Stock prices would rebound. But he was afraid Dana's trust never would.

On Monday morning, Dana took the triplets to BabyCare. She was still basking in the glow of a wonderful weekend, the highlight of which was Quentin's kiss. She'd understood his motive and thrown herself into it. Almost instantly she'd forgotten that anyone was watching. When he'd pulled away, she'd almost told him to forget the stupid promise and kiss her again.

But that was fantasy; she had to deal with real life. The kids dropped their coats and ran to the toy corner. Thank goodness they loved it here. As strong-willed as they were, if they were unhappy life would be hell. But this environment, with its craft tables, toys and primary colors galore was safe and nurturing. It met all her maternal standards. And was fun for the kids.

She noticed a volunteer named Emma playing with Sammy and Steffie, the abandoned twins. The two were cute as could be with their strawberry-blond hair and blue eyes. Dana marveled at how much children learned in their first year. When they'd been left, the babies were sitting up and crawling. Now they were standing and taking tentative steps. While the volunteer watched over them. In fact Dana had noticed that about Emma every night when she picked up her own children.

Upon Emma's arrival in town almost two months ago, she'd been mugged and lost her memory after she'd fallen in a struggle with the thief. Sheriff Malone had found out the mystery woman's first name because of a necklace with ''Emma'' engraved on it that she wore around her neck. But as far as Dana knew, the woman hadn't regained her memory.

There was so much Dana would like to forget—like her former husband's indifference and unfaithfulness. Not to mention her present husband's attentive sweetness. And his kisses.

He'd explained the kiss in the pumpkin patch was to distract the reporter and protect their marriage of convenience for the sake of the custody battle. But it had certainly distracted Dana, too. There had been a desperation in the touch of his lips on hers that she didn't understand. Yet that very quality reached out to her, tugged at her, made it impossible to forget how her heart had pounded and sent heat radiating through her.

Emma noticed her there and smiled. She settled the twins with activity toys and joined her.

''Hi, Dana.'' Her green eyes sparkled with pleasure. Red curls skimmed her shoulders and danced around her pretty face.

''Hi. How's it going?''

''Okay, for a woman who can't remember her own name.''

Dana shook her head sympathetically. ''I hope Tucker

catches the mugger who did this to you and locks him up and throws away the key."

"I'm not sure that's Tucker's style, the throwing away the key part. But take it from someone who knows, possessions can be replaced, but you don't know how precious memories are until they're gone."

Dana sighed. "You're right. I was just watching you, thinking about things I'd like to forget. But I realize that all of our experiences shape us. Lessons learned are important so we don't make the same mistakes—"

Dana suddenly realized that Emma wasn't listening. Her attention was fixed on Sammy and Steffie and there was a glazed look in her green eyes.

Dana waited a moment, not knowing what to do. Then she touched the other woman's arm. "Emma? Are you all right?"

"What?" Emma blinked several times. Then she rubbed her temple with her fingertips as she focused on Dana. "Did you say something?"

"You zoned out there for a minute. Are you okay?"

"I had a vague memory of hanging baby clothes on a line."

"That's wonderful." Dana looked closer and noticed the frown on her face. "Isn't it?"

"I don't know," Emma said, a note of desperation in her voice. "After I hit my head, the doctor examined me and said I've never had children. So why would I be hanging baby clothes on the line?"

Dana touched her arm. "I wish I knew. I wish I could help."

"The neurologist says it will just take time. I need to be patient," she said, grimacing as she massaged both temples now.

"Are you in pain?" Dana asked.

"I get flashes, but I don't know how the pieces fit. Then the headache comes."

"Can I get you something?"

Emma shook her head. "The doctor prescribed medication. I'll take it when I get home—I mean Aunt Gertie's. That's where I'm staying."

Uncomfortable, Emma turned away and started to straighten the magazines and reading material in the waiting area. She picked up the morning newspaper and pulled off the protective plastic. Then she glanced at the headline and froze.

"What is it?" Dana asked. "Are you having another memory?"

"I can't believe this," Emma said, staring at the newsprint. She turned and studied Dana. "Have you seen the newspaper today?" she asked as if there was something in it that should matter to her.

Dana laughed. "I don't see it any day. But I got an especially early start today. We left before the paper was delivered. What's wrong?"

"Nothing," Emma said putting it down. "Forget it."

Dana reached for it. "Something in it got your attention. I guess if it was a natural disaster, I would already know. But—"

When she read the headline, all the air left her lungs. It was a disaster, all right. But not natural. The story was about Quentin.

"Saint or Sinner? Generosity or Guilt?" the headline screamed, right above her husband's picture. The article was worse; it implied that Quentin was the father of the abandoned twins.

Chapter Eight

Monday morning Quentin walked into his office on top of the world. The weekend had been great. The highlight was kissing Dana in the pumpkin patch. The good news was that since he hadn't promised, he hadn't broken his word. More good news was that she'd thanked him for thinking fast to protect her kids. He would do whatever he could for them.

But he was no plaster saint. He'd enjoyed the hell out of that kiss. And if the rest of the weekend was anything to go by, Dana had, too. They were getting closer. He could feel it.

Life was good.

"Top of the morning, Doleen. Isn't it a wonderful day?"

"You really think so?" she answered doubtfully.

"I do, indeed. Don't you?" He looked at her tense expression. "Why wouldn't it be?" he asked, puzzled.

Before she could answer, the phone rang. "Mr. McCormack's office. Hold, please." She pushed the button and looked at him. ''I guess you haven't seen the paper this morning.''

He'd been running late. Overslept. Thoughts of Dana, the pumpkin-patch kiss and the rest of their weekend, spent together with the kids. He'd tossed and turned until the wee hours. He wanted Dana; he wanted a family. And the big question—how could he convince her to stay?

Things between them had happened fast, but it was right. Just like he'd told that nosy reporter.

''I didn't have time to look at the paper,'' he confessed.

''It will take you about a second and a half to read the headline. That will be enough to ruin your morning.'' She took the newspaper from her desk and handed it to him. The phone rang again and she put the caller on hold.

She was right. One glance at the headline was enough to ruin his day and maybe his whole life. With Dana. His blood ran cold when he skimmed the story below. Barbara Kyle *had* dug and hit pay dirt. If she'd written lies, he could sue for libel. Unfortunately, everything in the article was the truth. He'd never been so angry and frustrated in his life. And worried.

A minute ago, he'd wondered how he could convince Dana to stay. Now he questioned whether or not it was even possible. One of his rationalizations for marrying her was to help with damage control if this story ever got out. Well, it was out. He would need a miracle to salvage his image with her.

He looked at his secretary. ''Doleen, hold the fort. I have to see Dana.''

''Quentin,'' she said, her voice tight. ''I just put two

calls on hold. The first one is your attorney. The second is your public-relations director."

"All right. I'll take them in my office. Then I have to talk to Dana."

Late that evening, Quentin returned to the estate without managing to speak with his wife. The office phone rang practically nonstop and his public-relations person had advised him to talk. Silence was tantamount to an admission of guilt. His attorney had told him not to say anything except that the facts in the story were true, but slanted to make him look guilty. He should deny paternity and state that the DNA tests were due back any day and would clear him once and for all.

Every time he'd tried to leave the office, there had been an important call to take. He had tried several times to contact Dana at work, but had been told that she was unavailable. Did he dare hope that she hadn't seen or heard about the story? His last chance was for him to be the one to break the news to her.

He walked into the foyer and poked his head into the great room. His parents were sitting in the hunter-green wingback chairs before the cheery blaze crackling in the fireplace. They were having drinks. A bad sign, since the strongest beverage they usually had was orange juice.

"Hi," he said. "Is Dana home?"

His mother nodded. "She's upstairs putting the children to bed."

"Thanks." He started to turn away.

"Quentin, what's all this nonsense about?" Carter asked. The worry in his father's voice was unmistakable.

He sighed. As anxious as he was to see his wife and

make everything all right, he knew he owed his parents an explanation.

He walked into the room. "It's not true."

Amanda stood up and walked over to him. She hugged him tight. "We know that. But what's going on?"

"A couple of weeks ago, Tucker Malone came to see me about the rattle that was found with the twins. He recognized the McCormack crest on it and asked if I knew anything about it."

"Why would you? It's from a display of heirlooms in one of the upstairs guest rooms. At least it was."

He nodded. "I told the sheriff that I would check with you to see if you'd noticed anything missing."

She shook her head. "But they're not under lock and key. Anyone would have access—visitors, guests, staff."

"That's what I told him," Quentin confirmed. "I never asked you because I didn't think this whole thing would amount to a hill of beans and would only cause you needless concern."

His mother looked worried. "By itself, the rattle would be nothing. But along with your donation to BabyCare, where the children were left, it looks bad."

"How did that information get out?" he asked.

"Not a clue," his mother said.

He nodded. It didn't really matter anyway. The damage was done. "I want you both to know that I didn't father those children. If I had, I would take responsibility—"

Carter snorted disdainfully. "You don't have to tell us that, son." He stood up and joined them in the doorway. "What we would like to know is how Dana fits into the picture."

"What do you mean?"

"Is it a coincidence that this story breaks and late today she received a special-delivery letter from a law firm in Omaha?"

"In your diplomatic way, you're asking why Dana and I married suddenly." Quentin let out a long breath. "I proposed the day she found out her former in-laws were suing her for custody of the triplets."

"No," his mother gasped. His father just looked grim.

"The coincidence is that it was the same day Tucker confronted me about the rattle. I thought that a family-man image would help with company damage control if the suspicions got out. We decided that united we stand, divided we—"

His mother nodded. "I had a feeling there was more to it than what you'd told us."

"I'm sorry, Mom. I should have given you all the facts but I didn't want you to—"

"Worry. Yes, I know," she said with a small smile as she touched his cheek. "And I love that about you."

"I'm sorry you're disappointed in me," Quentin said, meeting his mother's gaze.

"Don't be ridiculous. I've never been disappointed in you. Not a single minute, hour, or day of your life. And I'm proud now." A fierce look replaced the tenderness in her expression. "It just burns me up that a good deed can be twisted into something negative and ugly."

Quentin stuck his hands in his trousers pockets. "They say no good deed goes unpunished."

"That's a stupid expression and I don't understand it," she said. "But there's something I do know. You can tell yourself marrying Dana was a good deed. Or that it was for business reasons. And she can claim it was for the children. But I know there's something deeper than that."

Carter kissed her and put his arm around her shoulders. "Did you know your mother is psychic?" he asked jokingly.

"She's been saying that for years," Quentin agreed.

She slanted him, then Carter, a mock glare. "You two can scoff if you want. And for the record, I never claimed to have ESP. But I've got e-y-e-s. And that's all I'm going to say," she said. "Now go talk to your wife. She looked upset when she came in. I'm sorry we delayed you this long."

Quentin kissed her cheek, shot his dad a grateful look, then took the stairs two at a time. When he reached Dana's suite, he noticed that her door was open slightly. Nudging it gently, he stepped inside. Just in time to see her backing out of the children's' room. He heard Lukie say, "Wanna see Mr. Mac."

"He's working late tonight, sweetie," Dana answered.

Was there an edge to her voice? Or was his imagination working late too?

"No he's not," Quentin said.

She whirled around. "I didn't hear you come in." She put a hand to her chest. "You startled me."

"Sorry." More than anything, he wanted to take her in his arms and hold her. To make this nightmare go away. But all he said was, "I'll say good-night to the kids. Then I need to talk to you."

He wanted to hear her say there was nothing to talk about. That she didn't for one moment believe he could turn his back on his own children.

But all she said was, "Okay."

He went into the room and Lukie sat up in bed. "Mr. Mac! You're home."

"Hi," Molly said. In the light from the doorway he could see her mole. And her smile.

"Hi," Kelly said with a grin. By process of elimination he knew it was her. "You missed baf time."

"I know." He made the rounds, kissing each one of the children. "Sorry, you guys. It was a bad day." And likely to get worse, he thought. He sat down on Lukie's bed.

"Need a hug?" the boy said holding out his arms. "Mommy hugs me when I feel bad."

"Yeah," Quentin said, taking the child in his arms.

"All better?" Lukie asked.

"All better, buddy," he answered, a catch in his voice. "Now you guys do as your mom says and get some sleep."

"We will," they replied together.

He left the door ajar and joined Dana in the sitting area. "Sorry I'm late. It's been a brutal day."

"You don't say?" She was standing on the far side of the room with her arms wrapped around her waist.

"Mom told me about the special delivery from the Omaha law firm. What's up?"

"The hearing's been moved up. It's the Friday before Halloween."

He ran his fingers through his hair as he let out a long breath. "Damn. The timing couldn't be worse."

"You're right about *that*."

Her emphasis on the one word told him there was a whole lot he wasn't right about. Then he noticed the newspaper on the coffee table. "You saw." It wasn't a question.

"Yes."

"You're upset." Also not a question.

"Why should I be? You told me about the DNA test."

"It looks bad, I know."

"Because your rattle was found with the twins? And you donated a lot of money to the day-care center where they were left? That's all circumstantial."

Why did her words *not* make him feel better? "That's true."

"According to the paper's anonymous source, better known as dispatcher Cora Beth Harper, the sheriff questioned you several weeks ago." She tucked a mahogany strand of hair behind her ear. "Which means you knew about this when you proposed."

"Yes, but that's not the real reason I—"

She held up a hand to stop him. "You don't owe me an explanation, Quentin. We both had our reasons for marrying. And we took steps to protect ourselves. End of story." She stuck her shaking fingers in the pockets of her jeans.

He wanted to tell her that there wasn't a lawyer on earth who could draw up a legal document as protection for what ailed him. But she wouldn't want to discuss that, either.

In fact the whole situation was even worse than he'd imagined. She was so sure she couldn't trust him, she'd shut down. She didn't even want to talk about it. Why now, when he'd lost any chance with Dana, did he realize how very much he wanted her in his life? He couldn't stand by and do nothing.

"It's not the end of the story, Dana. Just the beginning." He needed that to be true. "My reputation is slimed. Tucker Malone promised to keep his investigation quiet to prevent this."

"Define *this.*"

"Personal scandal—true or not—affects the company stock. By tomorrow, McCormack shares will be in the dumper. Investors will lose money. Some of those investments belong to folks who are counting on the money for retirement or to fund their kids' college." A muscle in his cheek contracted. "I was so sure it would blow over that I didn't even say anything to my folks. Besides, I figured the fewer people who knew, the better the chance that the DNA results would be back before any suspicions became public knowledge."

"So what about the DNA test?" she asked tightly.

"It will be another week and a half before the report is back. My office has already issued a press release. Some people will believe me." He prayed she would fall into that category. "Some won't. Despite what the law says, a person isn't always considered innocent until proven guilty. The press can be judge, jury and executioner. A lot of damage could be done before I have proof of my innocence."

And not just to his investors, he thought, looking at her face. If she was angry, he would take that as a positive sign. If she displayed emotion, he'd know that she cared. But her absence of feeling worried him.

Because he was in love with her. More every day.

Hell of a time to realize it. Really bad timing. Still, it was on the tip of his tongue to tell her. But what was the use? She wouldn't believe him if he stripped down to his skivvies and shouted it from the roof of the *Storkville Sentinel*.

He'd never opened himself to the emotion because he'd learned that affection usually rose and fell in conjunction with his bank balance. But Dana had stormed his defenses because she was the *right* woman. Only his right woman had been wronged by a dishonorable man.

He shook his head. "I hate that I'm paying the price for what your ex-husband did."

‘‘This has nothing to do with Jeff.’’

‘‘It has everything to do with him. He turned you into a skeptic who doesn’t trust your own shadow.’’

She looked away and clenched her teeth for a moment before answering. ‘‘The article raises a lot of questions about you.’’

‘‘You said yourself that it’s all circumstantial evidence. The way it was written, Mother Teresa would look guilty.’’

‘‘By definition, she couldn’t be a father,’’ she said with a small smile.

‘‘You know what I mean. The facts are correct,’’ he said. ‘‘The conclusion is wrong.’’

‘‘You told me once that you’re not irresponsible about birth control.’’ She let the statement hang there, as if she expected him to say something.

‘‘That’s true,’’ he finally answered.

He waited for her to tell him she believed him, trusted him, had unconditional faith in him. The first time he’d met Dana, he’d known she was different from any other woman. He’d thought she was the one who would see him for the man he was and care about him for himself. As her silence stretched out, he realized that he’d had no idea being wrong would hurt this much.

‘‘Quentin, to be honest, I’m not sure what to believe.’’

The words fell far short of what he’d wanted to hear. ‘‘I’d hoped you would believe that there was no way I could be the father of those babies.’’

‘‘So you’re not even going to try to convince me?’’

‘‘What good would it do, Dana? You’ve told me that words aren’t good enough for you. But all of my actions apparently don’t mean a tinker’s damn. You still believe the worst.’’

‘‘I never said—’’

"You didn't have to say anything. All your actions have shown me what you believe." He moved to the door and put his hand on the knob. "Sometimes, Dana, words *and* actions aren't enough. Sometimes you just need to take a leap of faith based on nothing but gut instinct." He waited a moment. "I guess there's nothing more to say."

The next day at work, Dana felt more alone and confused than ever before in her life. Her gut said that Quentin wasn't the twins' father. Her head told her she would be a fool to believe in him given the facts. She was straightening a rack of toddler-sized Halloween costumes when the bell over the door rang. She looked up to see Hannah Caldwell walk in.

When the woman spotted Dana, she smiled and walked over to where she was working. "Hi, Dana."

"Hannah." She braced herself. All morning customers had been looking at her curiously. No doubt wondering about her husband. She figured the day-care owner was no exception and they knew each other well enough for her to ask Dana what was going on. "What can I do for you?"

"I need to replenish my stock of disposable diapers, all sizes. Training pants and assorted T-shirts and play pants too. I hope you've got a sale in progress. These are just extras for those unexpected emergency spills that kids always have."

"Oh, I see you've met my Lukie," Dana said trying to ease the tension with humor. "It wouldn't surprise me if he's responsible for ninety-five percent of your emergencies."

Hannah laughed, but Dana felt like bursting into tears. She couldn't help remembering that her son's spills had helped her meet Quentin. With each day that had passed since then, her attraction to him had grown stronger. As deep as her feelings were, she couldn't believe that they'd only known each other so short a time. Heaven one minute, hell the next because a news story had shattered her world.

"I think what you want is over here," she said, leading the other woman to the clearance table.

"How are you and Quentin doing?" Hannah asked, her tone casual as she dug through the clothes.

"All right." Dana didn't pretend to misunderstand.

"I didn't know he was the mysterious benefactor." Hannah met her gaze. "But I'm glad I finally found out."

"Why?" she asked. That information had turned her own world upside down. How could Hannah be glad?

"So I can thank him. Because of his generosity, I was able to open my doors much sooner than I planned. It's a service Storkville families—mothers in particular—badly needed."

"I'm three times as grateful as any mother in this town," Dana said fervently.

"Then you need to thank your husband."

"You don't believe he's the father of the twins?"

Sun-streaked brown hair danced around Hannah's face as she shook her head. Her brown eyes took on a burning intensity. "Absolutely not."

"How can you be so sure?"

"Barbara Kyle's article twisted Quentin's generosity so that it appeared his motivation was a guilty conscience. First of all, I received the money before BabyCare opened, which was before the twins were left there."

"I hadn't thought about that," Dana admitted. She'd

been too stunned, not to mention worried about the upcoming hearing, to look at the situation calmly.

"You don't put any credence in that article, do you?" Hannah asked.

"Quentin has never said or done anything that would lead me to believe he would turn his back on any children he'd fathered," she said truthfully. "Why else do you believe Quentin is innocent?"

"It just doesn't make sense that he would have given me the money for the center as payment for the twins. We could have turned the babies over to the county. There's no way Quentin or anyone else could have known that Jackson and I would take the twins home with us."

"For how long?"

Hannah nodded and a sweet smile brightened her face. "We will keep them as long as we can."

"You don't want to give them up?"

"No."

"What if the sheriff finds the person who abandoned the babies? How do you feel about that?" Dana asked.

"I'm not sure. That's something I can't answer until it happens. *If* it happens. In spite of the town legend about the stork, children have fathers and mothers, aunts, uncles and grandparents. I believe it's very important for them to know their family, to have a sense of where they came from." She sighed and shook her head. "It's so complicated. Mostly I try to take it one day at a time and not borrow trouble."

Dana nodded. "I know what you mean."

Together they sorted through the clearance-priced clothes until Hannah had emergency outfits in several different sizes without being gender specific.

Dana rang up the sale and bagged the merchandise. "If there's anything else you need, just let me know."

"Thanks, Dana. Tell Quentin I said hi. And don't worry about the stupid suspicions. It will blow over. Don't let it ruin what you and Quentin have."

"I'll tell him."

But would it blow over?

The other woman walked out the door and passed the store window on her way back to the day-care center. Dana wanted to believe that Quentin was telling her the truth. Was he right? Was he paying the price for what Jeff had done? She didn't want to believe the man she'd married was capable of this. The triplets adored him and he seemed to genuinely return the feelings. It was almost impossible to accept that a man who embraced her kids more profoundly than their own father, could turn his back on his own flesh and blood.

And her growing feelings? Everything had happened so fast. Could she believe the instinct that told her Quentin was an honorable man? Could she trust her heart?

But, in spite of what Hannah had said, the two pieces of evidence against him were strong. She should have been more careful what she asked for. She'd almost wished for something to keep her from falling for him. Was it too late to take it back?

But Hannah had raised the most important question. What *did* she and Quentin have?

Chapter Nine

In worn jeans and T-shirt, Quentin walked into the kitchen at the crack of dawn on Saturday. On weekends, the cook didn't begin breakfast preparations until eight o'clock. So she left the automatic coffeemaker ready to go in case anyone got up early. He flipped the switch as he passed. While he listened to the sizzle and drip, he stared out the French doors to the expansive manicured lawn in back. There was a pool with a brick deck around it. Next summer he could teach the triplets to swim. They would have outdoor barbecues.

Then a single thought slammed him in the chest like a sledgehammer. Dana and the kids would be gone then.

"You're up early."

Dana's soft voice sliced through him and wrapped around his heart. He would miss hearing her, breathing in her sweet fragrance, seeing her sweet smile.

Closing his eyes for a moment, he braced himself, then turned to look at her. Mahogany curls framed her face in sexy disarray. She looked like she'd spent the night with a man who had run his fingers through her hair countless times. That man wasn't him and not likely to ever be, judging by the wary look in her gray eyes.

What a difference a week made. Seven short days ago, he'd kissed her in the pumpkin patch and almost elevated himself to hero status. Now he was the guy in the black hat.

"I couldn't sleep," he confessed.

"Me either."

They looked at each other for several moments and he missed the pre-scandal intimacy that had been growing between them. Did she miss it too? Why couldn't she sleep? Thinking about him? Regretting that she'd ever met him? If so, he was sorry that his bad press had cost her precious sleep. She looked tired.

The coffeemaker grew silent, making the room completely still. "Coffee?" he asked.

"Please," she said, nodding a little too eagerly.

Grateful to have something to do, he grabbed two mugs from the cupboard and poured the hot liquid into each. He handed one to her.

"Thank you," she said.

"You're welcome."

They were so damn polite. He'd like to take civility and throw it out the window. He'd like to take her in his arms and show her how much he cared. He ached to kiss her and run his hands through her hair until she looked twice as sexy as she already did.

But she backed away from him and his chest grew tight. There was a time when he would have made a joke about keeping a safe distance so she wouldn't spill on him. But he'd lost his sense of humor along with his good name. He was tempted to ask her if she believed in him, but he didn't want to hear the answer. He didn't mind losing what he already had, but he hated like hell that it had cost him Dana.

She blew on the coffee. "I'm taking the kids shopping for Halloween costumes today."

"They told me." They'd also begged him to go along.

"Molly and Kelly want to be Dorothy and Glinda the good witch from *The Wizard of Oz.*"

He nodded. "What about Lukas?"

"He doesn't know yet. He keeps changing his mind."

"They were pretty excited last night, about the shopping trip." The fact that he wouldn't be a part of it had kept him awake long into the night. "It should be fun."

She took a sip from her mug. "Would you like to go with us?"

His gaze snapped to hers. He couldn't read her expression. "I'd like that very much. But are you sure?"

"I—I could use an extra pair of hands," she said carefully, looking at his. He thought she shivered slightly. "And it would mean a lot to the children," she added quickly.

Quentin was pleased. But as the clouds drifted through her gray eyes, he couldn't help feeling that she didn't think he would do it for her.

"I'd be happy to give you a hand. And I would do anything in my power to give the triplets whatever they want," he said, meaning every word.

If only it were in his power to turn the clock back and make everything the way it was before the story broke. The triplets had been thriving in the stable two-parent environment. But they had been more demanding in the last week, more clingy with their mother.

They felt the tension, even if they didn't understand what was going on. Half of Storkville looked at him as if he were a serial killer and the other half vigorously defended him. The Hatfields and McCoys. He just wished he knew which camp Dana pitched her tent in.

"I thought we could go early, before the stores get crowded," she said.

There was his answer. Guilty as charged. She wanted his help with the kids, but the fewer people who saw her with him the better. "Whatever you want."

"You should know what you're getting into before you fully commit to this. It could take all day. You'd be surprised how opinionated three-year-olds can be about what's exactly right for their costume."

His spirits rose at her words. All day? Did that mean she wasn't concerned about being seen with him? "We can take all the time they need."

She sent him a sweet, grateful smile. "I'll go get ready while they're still sleeping."

He knew it was setting himself up for a fall, but her expression encouraged the small kernel of hope in his soul. "Let's synchronize our watches. Meet you back here at eight-thirty?"

"Okay."

Before Dana and the kids his life had been empty. He knew it would be again. But, God help him, today he would make the most of his time with them. He would never be ready to let them go. But he was grateful to have another memory to add to his precious, pitifully small stash.

Around noon, Dana sat down on the bench in the center of the mall and let out a long, weary breath as she watched shoppers hurry by. She looked at Quentin as he dropped beside her. As always, desire curled through her at his nearness. She kept waiting for the feeling to go away. But, in spite of his daily negative press, her attraction grew stronger. He'd been wonderful with the children today. If it was an act, it was a darn good one. The man had the patience of Job and tenacity that was a match for the most persistent three-year-old.

Whatever his reason, she enjoyed his company. More than she should. And she was grateful for his help.

"Thanks to you, the girls are all set. If you hadn't found those ruby slippers..." She leaned close and whispered conspiratorially, "The red glitter is our little secret."

Her stomach flip-flopped at his grin. "As far as I'm concerned, those shoes came straight from Oz," he whispered back.

"Now we just have to get Lukie squared away." She glanced at the children who were chasing each other just a few feet away. "Lukie, come here sweetie."

The boy ran over to her. "What, Mommy?"

"Can you tell me what you want to be for Halloween?"

"Yes, I can," he said.

"Don't let his decisiveness fool you. We have to narrow down the choices," she explained to Quentin. Then she said to her son, "Do you want to be a fireman, or the space guy?"

The boy looked from her to Quentin. "Want to be Mr. Mac," he said nodding his head emphatically.

That didn't startle her as much as she would have thought. Kids wanted to emulate their hero on Halloween. In her son's eyes, Quentin wore the red cape, blue tights and had a capital *S* on his chest. As far as she was concerned, he had done everything right, too. Once that would have been enough to guarantee her trust. She would have dismissed the suspicion that he was the twins' father as ridiculous. But that was before her first husband had used her hero-worship against her.

Now one minute she thought there was no way Quentin could have done what the newspaper implied. The next, doubts crept into her mind. She'd been wrong once. Was she mistaken again?

She took her son's hands. "You want to wear a suit and tie for trick or treat?" The boy nodded solemnly.

When she met Quentin's gaze, she saw his pleased smile and the sparkle in his eyes. So his next words were a surprise.

"That's really nice, buddy. But we saw that great fireman's helmet in the toy store. And the playset with the hose and hatchet and badge. Don't you think that would be more fun?"

Lukie looked torn. After several moments of thought and shifting from one foot to the other, he said, "Wanna be Mr. Mac." Then he ran off to chase his sisters again.

Quentin looked at her. "If he could read, he probably wouldn't feel that way."

"He's too young to understand," she agreed. "Kids are impressionable."

"So are adults," he said pointedly, the blue in his eyes growing more intense as he let his words sink in.

"Quentin, I don't know—"

He held up his hand. "Let's not rehash it. There's nothing more to say. Besides, I have a great idea. About Lukie's costume," he clarified.

"What?"

"Let's get him a suit. Unless he's already got one, he'll need it anyway for the hearing."

"He doesn't have one." For a little while she'd managed to forget about the looming legal battle. Her stomach clenched at the reminder.

Quentin must have seen the fear and dread in her eyes. He reached over and squeezed her hand. "Sorry. I didn't mean to spoil your mood."

"Don't worry about it," she said, savoring the warmth of his touch. "It's always in the back of my mind. It takes so little to bring it to the surface."

He threaded his fingers through hers and rested their joined hands on his solid thigh. "We'll be ready. My lawyer will be there. It'll be fine. You'll see."

"I know." She had difficulty controlling the shiver of awareness that rolled through her. He was so very male. With an effort, she turned her thoughts back to the current problem. Luke's costume. "So if we get him a suit, what if he changes his mind at the last minute?"

"I thought that was a woman's prerogative. Molly and Kelly were quite adamant about what they wanted to be."

"Apparently Lukie got my indecisive gene."

"What does that mean?" he asked.

"Nothing," she said, not wanting to go where that would take them. "The point is, Halloween night will be too late to put together another costume if—"

"If I let him down. If the DNA test comes back and says I fathered the twins." His mouth pulled tight and his blue eyes darkened with anger as he jumped to the wrong conclusion.

"No. That's not what I meant."

"Sure it is. Not that I blame you. Under the circumstances unconditional faith is too much to ask."

"Quentin, that's not fair. I—"

"Forget it. I'm sorry. I guess it's uppermost in my mind too. Back to the problem at hand. Let's get Lukie the fireman outfit *and* the suit," he said, quickly changing the subject.

"I can't afford two costumes."

"I can." His look was endearingly sincere. "Let me, Dana. I wouldn't offer if I didn't want to. Things have been pretty tense lately. Look at us just a minute ago. I know the kids sense it. I want to put the smiles back on their faces."

She studied his expression. If he had an ulterior motive, she couldn't see it. He seemed to genuinely want to do it. And she had a feeling when trick-or-treat time rolled around, Lukie would want to be a fireman. Even if the DNA results went against Quentin, Lukie was too little to understand his hero's fall from grace. Positive or negative, soon he would have to leave the man he'd come to worship. That was already going to break his heart. It would break hers if he was disappointed on Halloween too.

"If you're sure—"

"I am." He pulled her to her feet. "Let's go."

She pulled her hand from his. "Would you mind taking Lukie by yourself? He would love to have you all to himself. I'll take the girls into the stationery store. I want to get a card for the children to send their grandparents."

"The Hewitts?" he clarified, a frown on his face.

"I know what you're thinking," she said. "It's not to get in their good graces to make them reconsider the custody petition. I've always acknowledged them on holidays. And Hannah Caldwell said something that made me think."

"What was that?"

"Kids need to know their family, both sides. I can't change who their father was. Someday they might have questions only George and Beatrice Hewitt can answer. I just don't think it's a good idea to burn bridges."

He frowned. "You believe the worst about me, based solely on circumstantial evidence. But you're reaching out to the people who clearly and without a doubt are trying to take the kids from you." The anger on his face was unmistakable, along with his look of betrayal.

"I don't know how I feel," she said honestly. "But what can a card hurt?"

"Plenty."

"Quentin, it's just a card."

"And I'm guilty until proven innocent." He turned away. "Lukie, let's go get your costume."

Her son joyfully took his hand and together they walked through the mall crowd. Clearly Lukas was in no danger of a broken heart at the moment. But Dana felt her own crack. She hated herself for hurting Quentin like that. But she wouldn't lie to him, either. She wasn't sure how she felt about anything. Except she'd maxed out her fool limit once. She wouldn't do it again.

"Quentin, you don't have to go to the kids' costume party."

Across the street from the day-care center, Dana sat beside him in the car. Film crews had set up camp outside BabyCare. The stories about Quentin in the newspaper had garnered national attention, bringing more journalists to Storkville. He'd told her how he waded through cameras and microphones and a barrage of questions just to get into his office every day. The vultures were gathered now in hopes of seeing him at the children's Halloween party.

Quentin turned a chilly look on her. "If you're afraid to be seen with me, just say so."

"You know it's not that," she protested.

"Do I?" He laughed but there was no humor in the

sound. "Actually, I understand why you want to keep your distance."

"I'm concerned about you. I appreciate that you picked me up at the store for the party. But now that I see what you're facing, there's no need for you to run the gauntlet. The children will understand."

"Baloney. All they'll know is that I broke my promise to be there today. The only thing that could keep me from going in there is a natural disaster. Short of that, nothing can keep me away. Not even the bloodthirsty press out for their pound of flesh and the lead story on the six o'clock news."

"You're a good man," she said, touching his arm.

"Yeah?" The corners of his mouth curved up slightly. His expression held a flicker of warmth that chased away the chill from a minute ago.

"I wouldn't have said it if I didn't mean it."

He grinned. "Let's get it over with."

They got out of the car, and he took her hand. They crossed the street, then headed for the three-story Victorian house where the day-care center operated. The horde of reporters surrounded them, shoving microphones and tape recorders in their faces.

"Mr. McCormack, what's the status of the DNA test?"

"Are you the twins' father?"

"Have you got a statement for us, Mr. McCormack?"

Quentin turned at the top step. "Nothing has changed since I made my statement. That's all I've got to say."

"Mrs. McCormack, is there any truth to the rumor that you married Quentin to take the heat off him for turning his back on his own children?"

Inside, Dana started to shake. That had never occurred to her. She knew the proposal was sudden, but Quentin's explanation had made sense. Was he using her and the triplets? He'd said he wanted a hostess and cover from fortune hunters. He'd never claimed to love her. She wouldn't have believed him if he had.

But some part of her was affection-deprived. She wished for more from Quentin and wasn't sure why. That was a statement she couldn't make to the reporters.

Neither could she explain that she was using him, or rather his considerable legal resources, to maintain custody of her children. That could destroy her at tomorrow's hearing.

She looked at the mass of news media on the grass at the bottom of the steps. "No comment," she said.

As they turned away, Quentin took her elbow and guided her inside. In her ear he whispered, "Well done. Spoken like a tycoon's wife."

Not his wife for long, she thought. But the idea of a life without Quentin was empty and bleak and made her incredibly sad.

Her spirits lifted some as they went inside. The interior of the center was decorated for Halloween. Orange and black crepe-paper streamers scalloped the walls and crisscrossed the ceiling. Ghosts and witches were pinned up on bulletin boards along with the children's art work.

"Glad you could join us," Hannah greeted them. "Chairs are set up for the parents over there. Quentin, I hope you don't mind being our token dad. Most of the others are working and couldn't get away."

"I wouldn't have missed this for anything."

"Good," Hannah said. "Because we have a special celebration planned."

Dana and Quentin found a spot and sat. She couldn't help noticing that the tiny chair wasn't built for his solid six-foot frame. But he looked completely unselfconscious and so incredibly appealing that emotion clogged her throat.

While volunteers headed by Emma watched the babies and toddlers, Hannah lined the older kids up. They looked cute as could be in their costumes. Molly and Kelly were adorable as Dorothy and Glinda. There were ghosts, witches, and gypsies. A memo from Hannah to the parents had encouraged washable face paint rather than masks that could restrict the kid's vision and cause them to trip.

Hannah handed a rolled parchment paper tied with a white ribbon to Lukas.

"Okay, Lukie. You know what to do."

"Give this to Mr. Mac?" he asked.

"Can you do that?"

"Yes, I can," he said confidently.

In his three-piece pinstriped suit that was a tiny replica of what Quentin was wearing, Lukas walked over to them. He pushed the clear glass wire-rimmed spectacles up more securely on his nose.

"For you," he said, handing the scroll to Quentin. "Thanks for my pweschool."

"You're welcome, buddy," Quentin said. He slid Dana a puzzled look and she shrugged, telling him that she didn't understand what was going on either.

"Wead it," Lukas ordered.

"Yes, sir." Quentin slid the ribbon off and put it in his pocket. He unrolled the parchment and read, "'To Quentin McCormack with appreciation. Thanks to your donation, we have a safe place to play and grow while our parents are at work.' It's signed by all the kids," he said, angling it toward Dana so that she could see. There was a catch in his voice.

The words and childish printing tugged at her heart

and made the backs of her eyes sting with unshed tears. As the children sang the thank-you song that Hannah had taught them, Dana wanted to get the media in here. It was about time to publicize what a good thing he had done instead of crucifying him. But he'd made the donation anonymously. If he had wanted to capitalize on the gesture, he would have. He didn't want any fanfare.

Dana looked at him beside her. She took in the strong, masculine line of his jaw, and the way he swallowed several times, the only indication of his emotion. He *is* a good man, she thought.

She loved him.

Why hadn't she seen it before? Probably because she was trust-impaired. Not to mention that it all happened so fast. But it was true. And now that she'd acknowledged the feeling, it expanded like an airbag freed on impact. It grew bigger by the second. Along with her fear.

Infidelity and betrayal had destroyed the love she felt for her first husband. In spite of the ugly suspicions surrounding Quentin, she loved him.

This time, she had an awful feeling that nothing could kill it. If Quentin turned away from her the way Jeff had, it would destroy her.

Chapter Ten

The morning after the day care party, Dana sat on the sofa in her suite. She stared at the headline in the *Storkville Sentinel* and wondered if a jury of her peers would convict her for strangling a certain society-news reporter.

At the knock on her door, she called out, "Come in."

Amanda McCormack walked in. "Hi."

"Hi," she answered, stifling the note of surprise.

It had been three weeks since she and Quentin had married and she realized that his mother had never dropped in before. She'd had so much on her mind, Dana hadn't thought about the fact that his parents had respected their privacy. It was as if they were living in a separate residence.

She knew that after the story broke, Quentin had explained to his folks the circumstances surrounding their marriage. But she hadn't detected any shift in their manner from the kindness they'd shown in the beginning.

"Won't you sit down?" Dana invited, indicating the cushion next to her.

"Thank you." Amanda folded her hands in her lap and said, "Can we talk?"

"Of course. About what?"

"You and my son."

She looked at her mother-in-law. The kind expression on the woman's face softened the bluntness of her answer.

"What about us?"

"Why did you marry Quentin?"

"I thought he'd explained that. He said he could use a wife for business reasons and I needed his help to fight the custody petition initiated by my former in-laws."

"Yes, he explained things. Including the facts about your first marriage. You strike me as a young woman who would take her vows seriously. I want to know why you *really* got married. What is it about my son that convinced you to take the plunge again?" There was no hint of judgment or suspicion in her expression. She merely seemed curious and concerned about her son, like any mother.

"Quentin was kind to a three-year-old boy who trashed his expensive trousers."

"Anything else?"

"He took time from his busy day and attended a children's Halloween party at the day-care center because a three-year-old boy who's lonely for a man's influence asked him to. And he wouldn't break his promise. Even—"

"Go on."

She took a deep breath. "Even though he knew the press would have a field day with it. 'Hiding behind a woman's skirts,' indeed." Angrily, she tossed down the paper. "'Wolf in sheep's clothing,'" she scoffed. "They think their headline is so clever—Halloween references and everything. It really makes me mad.''

''Me too.''

''Implying that he married me only to improve his public image. They practically came right out and said that's why he was at the party.'' She looked at the other woman. ''I wanted to tell them about the certificate of appreciation Hannah gave him, signed by all the children.''

''But he won't let you.''

''No,'' Dana confirmed. ''He shows up and they twist it into something false and ugly,'' she said adamantly.

''You don't have to convince me. I'd like to cut Barbara Kyle's heart out with a spoon.''

Dana stared at her, then couldn't help laughing. ''Never underestimate a mother's wrath.''

''Exactly.''

Dana sighed. ''If it weren't for the rattle and his donation… Those two pieces of evidence are incriminating—''

''Do you have doubts?'' Amanda asked sharply.

''No.'' She met the other woman's intense gaze. ''I don't know.'' Dana threw up her hands in frustration. ''The rattle?''

''It was not under lock and key, but prominently displayed in the house. Anyone could have taken it. Besides, it doesn't mean a thing.''

''It has the McCormack crest on it,'' Dana said.

''But Quentin isn't a McCormack. Not by blood,'' she added.

Dana was stunned. ''But he uses the name.''

''It's legally his. Carter adopted him after we were married.''

''It never occurred to me. I thought—''

"That Carter is his father?"

She nodded. "He calls him Dad."

"He is, in every way that matters," Amanda said. "But the rattle is not his. Even if he'd fathered the twins, he wouldn't have given them a keepsake he wasn't entitled to."

"What about the donation to BabyCare?" Dana looked at the other woman. "Why would a bachelor, who *didn't* have any children, give such a generous amount of money to a day-care center?"

Amanda's mouth pulled to a straight line and there was an expression of remembered pain in her eyes. "Because he knows what it feels like to have a working mother. Before I married Carter, Quentin was a lonely latchkey kid before the term was even popular. He knows firsthand how important safe and nurturing child care is and genuinely wanted to help Hannah get her business off the ground."

"Why keep it a secret?"

"He hates publicity, and I believe you can see why," she added wryly. "And he truly didn't want any recognition."

"That's very like Quentin to keep it quiet." Dana's head was spinning as she tried to make sense of this new information.

"How did you and Carter meet?"

Amanda smiled and there was a dreamy, faraway look in her eyes. "This will sound like a cliché. I took a clerking job in his company. I caught the boss's attention."

"How romantic," Dana said.

"Not entirely. I had a son and hardly two pennies to rub together. His family thought I was after his money."

"I know how that feels," Dana admitted. "So that's

where Quentin gets his opinion about fortune-hunting women.''

''No. His conviction is based on his own experience.''

In so many ways, Dana felt as if she'd known Quentin forever. It suddenly became clear that she knew very little about him. That didn't change her mind about the fact that he was the most decent man she'd ever met. But learning how he'd turned out that way was fascinating.

''Tell me about his experiences,'' she pleaded.

''When I started my job at McCormack, Incorporated, Quentin was thirteen, an age when kids can be incredibly cruel. My priority was food on the table for a boy growing so fast he practically inhaled it. His peers judged who to befriend by what designer label was on their jeans.''

''I remember. It was the same for me in school,'' Dana said angrily. ''The only good thing about those years is the character they built.''

''Well, Quentin has lots of that.'' Amanda smiled. ''He wore generic jeans to school. No designer labels or famous brand-name shoes for him. It broke my heart that I couldn't afford them. Girls used to tease him and he just took it. Boys would taunt him until the situation escalated into a fight.''

''How awful.''

''Anyone a little different was a target. He'd come home with bruises and black eyes and make up stories about running into things. He's always been very protective of me. He didn't want me to worry. He was that way at thirteen and he's still the same at thirty-two.''

The images of what he'd gone through hurt Dana's heart. She ached for the boy he'd been. But instead of turning him into a bitter, cynical man, the experiences made him strong, kind and generous.

"So how did he come to the conclusion that if a woman was interested in him it was about his money?" she asked.

"After Carter and I married, he took Quentin shopping. Overnight his wardrobe improved," Amanda said with a smile. "The very next day girls started paying attention to him. Inside he was the same person, but suddenly expensive clothes an indication of money made everyone sit up and take notice of him."

"Shallow, selfish little witches—"

"You go, girl," Amanda said laughing. "Quentin was a teenage boy with a keen sense of fairness. He thought it stunk that anyone would be accepted just because they had money."

"So he learned that women care more about money and what it can buy than about him."

"It's a guess, but I know him pretty well. Which is why I understand his silence when these ugly accusations came to his attention. He's protecting Carter and me, his family."

"That's some character he built," Dana said sincerely. "When there's trouble he circles the wagons and hunkers down to take care of his own."

"It's what families do. They take care of each other."

Which is exactly the way Quentin treated her and the kids. A family from the first. Something she had never felt with Jeff, not in all the time they'd been together. She'd loved him from the beginning, but he'd managed to destroy her love.

"No wonder he was wary of women." Dana shook her head. "He and I have more in common than I first thought."

"How so?"

"We both judge first, ask questions later." She sighed.

"It's a shame other people have so much influence over us. Quentin's confidence took quite a beating when he was a boy."

"People lie, mirrors don't. Clothes don't make the man. How can Quentin not know that he's good-looking? Take it from me, he is, and it wouldn't matter if he wore thrift store or designer clothes. For that matter, beauty is only skin deep. He's also charming and funny and sweet and kind. And—what?" she asked when the other woman smiled knowingly.

"I can see why he never felt that you were after his money," Amanda said.

"You can?"

"You're in love with him." It wasn't a question. "In spite of all the hogwash printed about him. And he loves you."

Dana didn't know whether or not the slimy allegations swirling around him were true. But she knew she loved him in spite of them. But it was the part about Quentin loving her that got her attention. "What makes you think so?"

Amanda shook her head. "He can say he married you to plastic-wrap his image. But I know him. He's in love with you."

Before Dana could ask *how* she knew, the hunk in question walked into the room through his connecting door. He looked from one woman to the other.

"What's going on?" he asked.

"Love—" Amanda began, then stopped when Dana let out a high-pitched squeak. "*Love*-ly to see you, dear," she finished.

Good save. Maybe. Dana smiled at her mother-in-law.

"I don't mean to interrupt," he said, slanting both of them a quizzical look. "But I need to talk to Dana about the custody hearing this afternoon. There's been a development."

Dana's heart wrenched painfully. "What?"

"I'll leave you two alone," Amanda said standing.

"Wait, was there anything else?" Dana asked.

The other woman shook her head. "No. I got all the information I need." She gave Dana's hand a reassuring squeeze. "If there's anything I can do, don't hesitate."

After his mother left, Dana stared at Quentin, unable to tell whether it was a good development or bad. Make it good news, she prayed silently. She was feeling shaken by one revelation after another. Against all odds and in a shockingly short time, she'd fallen in love with Quentin McCormack. That knocked her for a loop. What other bombshell was he going to drop?

"I just got a call from the lawyer," he started, continuing to stand in the doorway.

Dana wished that he would sit beside her, that he would touch her. She'd never felt more alone. Having Quentin's strength to lean on had spoiled her. She wanted it now—and his warmth. But he'd been withdrawn ever since that stupid article had come out. She didn't blame him. Instead of defending him, she'd been indecisive, letting him conclude that she believed the suspicions. She'd told him that actions speak louder than words. Unfortunately, her behavior spoke volumes, and now there were no words to undo the damage.

"What did he say?" she asked.

"He's been in touch with the Hewitts' attorney. The judge assigned to the case wants a face-to-face meeting in chambers this afternoon."

"Is that good or bad?"

"I'm not sure," he admitted. "I'd say probably good, since the formality is cranked down a notch." He shrugged. "But depending on what comes out during the proceeding, who knows."

"What could come out?"

Anger pulled his mouth tight. "If their lawyer is any good, he'll bring up the suspicions surrounding me. He'll mention today's bad press and say I'm using you and the triplets to whitewash my public image."

"But the custody petition is about me. They have no right to drag you into this."

"A good attorney will make it about me. He'll attack your judgment. Barbara Kyle dug into our life, and came up with a story. A lawyer could do the same and figure out that you just married me to keep your kids."

"But now—"

"Maybe I shouldn't go," he interrupted. "If I'm not there to draw attention to the negative publicity, it might go better. You could lose your kids because of me." He dragged a hand through his hair.

"No. Why? How?"

"Think about it, Dana. You can't even say that you don't believe the allegations. How will that look to a judge?"

"I don't believe the allegations."

He gave her a skeptical look. "Right."

Dana found it *was* right. With her whole heart she knew he wasn't the kind of man who would turn his back on a child, especially his own. She'd known even before his mother had explained why he'd donated the money to the day-care center. But how was she going to convince Quentin that she was telling the truth? He would think she was like all those shallow high-school girls who didn't look beyond a designer label to the man inside.

He started to turn away, then he stopped and met her gaze. "Let me know if you want me there. Think it over carefully. I'll understand—whatever you decide."

Before she could tell him there was nothing to think about, she wanted him with her, he was gone.

Dana felt as if she was on the edge of losing everyone she cared about. If the Hewitts' attorney twisted the details of her marriage, her children could be taken away. And there was no way to prove that she truly believed in him and loved him.

Now she knew how very much she'd hurt him when she hadn't had the faith to believe that he was telling the truth.

Chapter Eleven

"He only wore this jacket for a few minutes at the Halloween party yesterday. How could he have gotten a spot on it?" she said to Quentin.

"Boys will be boys," he said, straightening Lukie's clip-on tie.

"Go downstairs wif girls?" the squirming little boy begged.

"Okay," Quentin said. "Go find your sisters."

Lukie grinned. "Be wight back." Then he raced out of the room.

Several hours after Dana's chat with Amanda, Quentin had dropped by her suite to help her get the triplets ready for the legal showdown. Dana studied him, so solid, so supportive in spite of the tension between them. And so handsome she could swoon like a schoolgirl with very little provocation. How could she, even for a moment, have entertained the notion that he could have done what the newspaper stories implied? More important, how had she ever gotten by without him?

In a short time, he'd become her Rock of Gibraltar. Not just because of the kids. He'd given boundless love a face and form.

How could she repair the cracks her doubts had made in their relationship? Miss Actions-Speak-Louder-Than-Words had really done it this time, she thought, kicking herself from here to Omaha. The average man would never have spoken to her again. But Quentin had proven time and again that he was above average—in kissing and everything else. Did she dare hope he would support her one last time in front of the judge?

She glanced at her watch. The confrontation with the Hewitts would take place in a couple of hours, but she was fretting even though they'd allowed generous driving time. It always took longer than she expected to get the children ready. Her eyes filled. She could lose them today and the man she loved, too. Quentin was convinced that she didn't trust him. She had weapons to fight for the kids—after all, she was their mother. No one could love them like she did. But Quentin…

"We have to get the kids there on time and spotless," Dana said, panic welling up again. She looked at him. "What if we're late? What if Lukie looks like he's being raised by wolves? What are we going to do—"

"We?" He met her gaze. "Does that mean you want me to come?"

"I don't think I could get through this without you," she said, pouring her heart into every word.

Dana knew quiet confidence was her best approach to convincing him she had no doubts about him. Wild declarations weren't her style and wouldn't ring true. "Do you *want* to come with us?" she asked.

Maybe he'd changed his mind. Had her uncertainty

cost her his support as well as his love? Her stomach dropped as she held her breath.

"I wouldn't miss it," he said simply. He pointed at Lukie's jacket. "Don't worry. That spot is hardly noticeable."

"Hardly means you can still see it. The judge will think I'm a horrible mother, dressing my son in dirty clothes. I have to—"

Quentin put his hands on her upper arms and looked into her eyes. "It means that Lukie is all boy and you're a wonderful mother for letting him be that." But he must have seen her anxiety because one corner of his mouth curved up and he said, "But if it will make you feel better, I happen to know from firsthand experience that there's some spot remover in the laundry room."

"You've certainly had occasion to use it since you met us," she said, smiling in spite of her nerves.

Part of her wondered how she could be so worried about a future with her children and at the same time want to kiss him. She wanted to feel his lips against her own and absorb his warmth, steal some comfort from him.

He gave her a reassuring squeeze before dropping his hands from her arms. "I'll round up the kids and get them in the car. You try to get the spot out of his jacket."

"Okay."

When he left her, Dana missed his reassuring presence. She felt that together they could accomplish anything. They were a dream team, at least in her dreams. When the custody issue hanging over her was settled—in her favor, she prayed—she planned to find a way to convince Quentin McCormack that she loved him. If he had been a bum living in a cave, she would still love him.

She hurried into the laundry room at the back of the big house and found the spray-on spot remover that Quentin had told her about. With a little rubbing, the stain was gone. When it dried, Lukie's little coat wouldn't look any worse for wear.

"Good." She nodded with satisfaction. "With a little luck, by tonight this custody thing will be nothing but a bad memory."

As she was hurrying through the house, one of the servants stopped her.

"Mrs. McCormack?" The maid had an envelope in her hand.

"Yes, Stella?"

"This special-delivery letter just arrived for Mr. McCormack. Can you see that he gets it?"

"Of course." Dana absently looked at the return address. The DNA results. Her heart lurched. This was what Quentin had been waiting for. After the maid walked away, she started to open the letter, even though she knew it would say that Quentin couldn't have fathered the twins.

Her hands stilled as an idea flashed into her mind. Her luck was changing for the better already. She'd been given a way to prove that she had unshakeable faith in Quentin. She took the still-sealed registered letter and slid it in the outside pocket of her purse.

She joined Quentin and the children who were waiting in the car. After closing the door behind her, she glanced back at the triplets and wished she didn't feel as if she were seeing them for the last time.

"When are we gonna get there?" Molly asked.

"Is it far?" Kelly wanted to know.

Her girls looked adorable in matching powder-blue coats and hats. Their little legs stuck straight out in front of them, giving her a good view of their lace-edged white socks and shiny black shoes. They were Sunday-school perfect.

"We gonna see Grandma Bea and G.G.?" Lukas asked.

"Yes," she said.

At bedtime the night before, she had prepared them as best she could for today. Quentin had helped. No matter what happened between them, she would be grateful to him as long as she lived for his voice of reason and calm manner with the kids. He'd been wonderful, as always. Again she wondered about the temporary state of stupid that had caused her to doubt him.

It was on the tip of her tongue to tell him she'd been an idiot, but now wasn't the time. She hoped with all her heart that she would have the opportunity to show him how much she loved and believed in him.

"Who's G.G.?" Quentin asked.

"Grandpa George," she explained.

"Went fishin' with G.G.," Lukas said.

"You were so little. I'm surprised you remember that." Dana glanced over her shoulder and studied her son. With this custody petition, she'd become angry and defensive toward her in-laws. She'd forgotten the good times, the positive things the Hewitts had done with the triplets.

From his place behind the wheel of the luxury car, Quentin looked at her. "Everything come out all right?" he asked, slanting a glance toward the little suit jacket in her lap.

She followed his gaze then and swallowed the lump

in her throat. "Like a charm. But it's a forty-mile drive. I think I'll hold on to this for safekeeping."

"There's no food or drink anywhere nearby," he said with a grin.

"This is Lukie we're talking about. I'm not taking any chances."

"It's going to be fine," he said, reaching over to squeeze her hand.

"I know," she answered, returning the pressure. She tried to tell him with that gesture how much she trusted him—with her children and her heart.

At the request of Judge Susan Warner, the children along with the lawyers waited in the reception area while Quentin and Dana and the Hewitts met in chambers. Quentin stood beside Dana's chair and studied the woman behind the desk. She was a tall, blue-eyed blonde and fortyish, which seemed too young to be making such a Solomon-like decision. He couldn't tell whether or not the fact that she was female would help their case.

She looked at them over the glasses perched on the end of her nose. "This is an informal session to avoid a court hearing if possible. I need to know why you're seeking custody of these children," she asked the Hewitts.

"My husband and I feel that we would be better suited to raise our grandchildren," Beatrice Hewitt said after a quick glance at the older man standing beside her.

She was an attractive woman in her mid to late fifties, dressed in a stylish and becoming tweed suit. Short, curly brown hair streaked with silver framed her round, relatively unlined face. Her husband was a distinguished-looking man, tall and gray-haired. Quentin saw a sadness in their eyes that he somehow knew went soul-deep.

"Why do you think the children would be better off with you?" the judge asked.

Mrs. Hewitt glanced at her former daughter-in-law, then met Quentin's gaze. She looked back at the judge. "Dana works full time. Up until a short while ago she was a single mother, barely able to make ends meet. My husband and I are well-off and could give the children the time, attention and care they need without relying on strangers—"

"Hannah's not a stranger. I know the day-care center director personally," Dana said, trying to defend herself to the judge.

"You'll have your chance to speak, Mrs. McCormack," the woman calmly interjected. She returned her attention to the Hewitts. "She's remarried now to Quentin McCormack, so I would assume money is no longer an issue. Nor is working. In this day and age there are many women who juggle careers and children as well as their marriages."

"Since you brought that up," Mrs. Hewitt continued, "George and I think she married him merely to obstruct our petition for custody. And according to the newspaper, he's suspected of being the father of the twins abandoned in Storkville. We believe they are not a committed couple, that the marriage is a sham. We're more convinced than ever that the triplets would be better off with us. A man like Quentin McCormack, who would shirk responsibility for his own flesh and blood, should not have influence over our grandchildren."

With his hand on her shoulder, Quentin felt Dana tense. He could feel the anger that shuddered through her. Then she leaned over to pull a sealed envelope from the side of her purse. She turned it over and looked at it, gripping it so hard the tips of her fingers turned white.

It was a registered letter from the medical lab. He was certain it contained the results of his DNA test and must have arrived just before they'd left the house. What was Dana planning to do with it?

"Your Honor, may I speak yet?" Dana asked.

"Yes."

"First of all," she began, glancing at her former in-laws. "It's true that Quentin and I married quickly. But as he once put it so eloquently, when it's right, why wait? I love him very much."

Quentin heard her quietly spoken words and knew she meant them for his benefit, not as a defense for her children. Relief washed over him. He could hardly believe his luck. She loved him! His heart swelled with hope that against all the odds, they might actually have a chance for happiness.

"What else, Mrs. McCormack?" the judge asked.

"I love my children with all my heart. So their custody is a highly emotional issue for me. When I received the notice of the petition, I was scared, as well as angry and defensive. On the way here today, my son reminded me that the children have happy memories with their grandparents. I'm sure Mr. and Mrs. Hewitt love them very much. But no one is better for them than their mother," she said emphatically.

"Is that all you have to say?"

"No, Your Honor." Dana handed her the sealed envelope. "My husband would never abandon a child, especially his own. And he's a supportive, strong and loving influence on the triplets. He took a DNA test in order to prove beyond a doubt that he did not father the twins. These lab results were delivered just before we left the house. This will substantiate his innocence."

"Dana?" he asked. "Are you sure?"

''Without a doubt,'' she answered, meeting his gaze as she reached up to squeeze the hand he'd rested on her shoulder.

Quentin couldn't believe it. She had handed over what could be the deciding factor in this custody case without looking to see for herself if he'd told the truth. Unless she had complete faith in him, Quentin knew she would never have done that. She was proving with her children's welfare that she believed in him without reservation.

He had never loved her more than he did at that moment.

He held his breath while Judge Warner read the results. She looked at him, then the Hewitts. ''This confirms that there's no possible way Quentin McCormack could have fathered those twins.''

Beatrice Hewitt let out a long breath as her shoulders slumped. ''That still doesn't change the facts of their marriage and why we believe it came about.''

The judge clasped her hands together and rested them on her desk. ''Too often I see children no one wants. I think these triplets are very lucky to have so many people who love them.'' The judge glanced at each couple. ''We could be here all day with charges going back and forth. But we haven't heard yet from the children.''

Beatrice Hewitt gasped. ''But they're hardly more than babies. How can they know what they want?''

''It's been my experience that children can't be fooled. They don't get caught up in words. They're too young to be prejudiced. They go on instinct. And I want to see how they feel. Bring them in, please,'' she said to Quentin.

He walked to the door and opened it. ''Come on in,

guys,'' he said. He looked at the attorneys who started for the chambers. ''Just the kids,'' he clarified.

Wandering around the waiting room, Lukas turned at the sound of his voice and raced to him. Quentin braced himself for impact.

''Hi, Mr. Mac. We been here a *long* time.''

''Yeah, buddy, but I think we're almost finished. There's someone who wants to see all of you,'' he said.

He put Lukas down and stepped back to usher the girls into the judge's chambers. Shyly, Molly and Kelly entered and glanced at the older couple. Lukas had crawled into Dana's lap and put his arms around her neck. ''Wanna go home, Mommy. Wif you and Mr. Mac.''

''He's so like Jeff,'' Beatrice whispered.

George let out a long breath. ''He's not our son, Bea. Jeff's gone, and it's wrong to try to bring him back through our grandchildren.''

Quentin looked at Beatrice Hewitt, who seemed to shrink before his eyes. Her body shook and she put a hand to her trembling lips. ''You're right. Oh, Dana. I—I can't go through with this,'' she said, shaking her head. ''I love them too much to take them away from their mother.''

Dana reached over and gripped her hand. ''What is it?''

Sniffling, the woman said. ''I miss my son. Their father.'' She looked at the judge. ''He was our only child. George is right. I was trying to get my son back by taking his children.''

''You don't need to take them,'' Dana offered. ''You can see them any time you'd like. I wouldn't try to keep them from you. And I believe with all my heart that they need you, too, to help keep the good things about their father alive.''

''He had his flaws,'' George Hewitt said. ''We ignored them and that was a mistake you paid for, Dana. I guess we were looking for a chance to make it right through the children. I'm sorry.''

''Forget it. We're not perfect. But we are family. And it's important that we all teach them, and show them their roots.''

''Well, I guess you don't need me anymore,'' the judge said, standing. ''If only all my cases were this easy,'' she added, with a smile. She walked to the door. ''Feel free to use the office as long as you need to.''

''Thank you, Your Honor,'' Quentin said.

''Molly, Kelly, Lukas, say hello to your G.G. and Grandma Bea,'' Dana said.

Lukas disengaged himself from her and wiggled off her lap. He walked over to the older man and looked up. ''Go fishin'?'' he asked.

There was a sheen of moisture in George Hewitt's eyes. ''You bet, son. But I think we'll have to wait till the spring thaw for that. Maybe we can go ice-skating instead,'' he suggested.

''He would love that,'' Dana said.

The girls looked up at their grandmother. ''They have Jeff's chin and mouth,'' she commented. ''People used to stop me on the street when he was little and tell me what a beautiful child he was.'' She stopped when her voice caught.

''I hope you'll tell the children about their father when he was a boy. You can give them so much that I can't.'' Dana held on to Quentin's hand as she used words to repair the rift with her in-laws.

George Hewitt absently ruffled Lukie's hair. ''Dana,

I'm so sorry for putting you through this. You too, Mr. Mc—''

''Call me Quentin,'' he said.

''That's very generous of you. We want very much to be part of the children's lives. All we ask is regular visits.''

''We'd like that,'' Dana said. ''You'll want to see the children dressed up for trick-or-treating.''

''Oh, yes,'' Beatrice said.

''I have an idea.'' Quentin met Dana's quizzical gaze. Then she squeezed his hand, telling him she trusted whatever he had in mind.

''Yes?'' Beatrice looked at him expectantly.

''Tomorrow night there's a costume party at the estate. Why don't you join us, stay for the weekend and through Halloween so that you can see the kids dressed up?''

''We couldn't impose—'' George started.

''It's not an imposition,'' Dana said. ''In fact, I think it's a wonderful idea.''

''Thank you. That's very generous.'' George held out his hand and squeezed Quentin's. ''We'll look forward to it. Won't we, Bea?''

''Without a doubt,'' the older woman concurred.

Doubt. Quentin thought about the word as he watched Dana hug her former mother-in-law. He couldn't wait to talk to his wife alone. They had some important things to discuss. Like tearing up their pre-wedding agreements.

Like making their merger a marriage.

Chapter Twelve

"I need to talk to you."

Standing in the pumpkin, ghost and goblin-garnished foyer, Dana turned at the sound of Quentin's voice. She watched him walk down the stairs. Her heart beat faster at the handsome figure he cut dressed as Rhett Butler for tonight's party. His parents had arranged their costumes and to complement Quentin's, she wore a long green-velvet hoop-skirted dress à la Scarlett O'Hara in *Gone With The Wind.*

"Ah do declare," she said, feigning a Southern accent as she batted her eyelashes at him when he stepped beside her. "Mistah Butlah, you are the handsomest thing."

"Thank you," he said grinning. He tugged the ends of his black string tie. Then he frowned and she could almost feel his frustration. "Don't distract me. Between dealing with your former in-laws, celebrating and tonight's festivities, we haven't talked since the judge's ruling came down. I can't wait any longer. And frankly my dear, I *do* give a damn."

Her heart fluttered as vigorously as her eyelashes just had. Since yesterday afternoon, she had hoped to tell Quentin two things: how sorry she was and that she loved him. If the gods were merciful, maybe he could find it in his heart to forgive her and love her in return.

But he was right. They hadn't managed to find time alone together. On the drive back, they'd had the triplets with supersonic hearing and curiosity in triplicate. After they'd arrived home, there had been a celebration with his folks. And from early that morning, they'd been going in different directions, getting ready for the annual estate costume party. She'd found a love that adversity couldn't kill. That was too important to discuss on the run.

"I can't wait, either." She brushed a hand down the front of his white shirt and black frock coat. He looked quite dashing. "Maybe we have a few minutes before guests start to arrive."

"Dana, you need to know—"

"Hi, Quentin. Dana." Tucker Malone walked into the room. "The maid let us in. You remember Emma."

"Of course," Dana said, smiling at the other woman. She was dressed as a Gypsy fortune-teller in a colorful peasant blouse and loose skirt. A fringed scarf tied around her hips accented her slender figure, while dangling necklaces and earrings finished off her attire. Her auburn hair was half-covered with a bandanna. "How are you?"

"Fine, considering I still can't recall my own name and I'm once again homeless."

"What happened? I thought you were living with

Aunt Gertie,'' Quentin said, slipping his arm possessively around Dana's waist.

She shivered at the contact. The rakish look he slid her told her that he'd felt her reaction. The expression was pure male, and it made her feel completely female—and not especially pure.

A wry look crossed Emma's pretty face. ''A whole boatload of her relatives descended on her without warning. She's very happy about it, but there's no room at the inn for me. And I wouldn't feel comfortable there under the circumstances.''

''I invited Emma to stay with me,'' Tucker interjected. ''Temporarily,'' he added.

''That's very nice of you,'' Dana said. ''You guys look great,'' she said to them.

Emma laughed. ''I'm hoping some of my Gypsy persona will rub off and I will look into my crystal ball and tell my own fortune. Or at least my name.''

Dana studied Tucker's jeans, boots and long-sleeved white shirt rolled to just below his elbows. ''Who are you supposed to be?'' she asked.

''Just myself,'' he said. But his face clouded. She had a feeling Tucker Malone out of uniform was a man confused about who he was and where he fit in.

''Hello, everyone,'' Amanda said. She and Carter walked into the foyer from the front room.

''Who are you guys supposed to be?'' Quentin asked. But the twinkle in his eyes said he was teasing.

Their elaborate attire was reminiscent of royalty. But it was the red hearts decorating their costumes that provided the big clue.

''It's not nice to tease the King and Queen of Hearts,'' his mother warned him. ''It's our job to give a nudge to couples on the brink of falling in love.'' She looked at

Tucker. "And I have a thing or two to say to you, buster."

"Mom, it's not politically correct or particularly wise to call the town sheriff *buster.*" Quentin's expression was wry.

Amanda raised an imperious eyebrow as she looked at her son. "You know, you're not on the smooth superhighway to love yet. And I know where your naked baby pictures are. I wouldn't be making fun of the Queen of Hearts if I were you."

"Don't say I didn't try, Tucker," he said.

Turning back to the sheriff, Amanda wagged her finger at him. "Now that the DNA results are back, I believe you owe my son an apology. How could you possibly think Quentin was the father of those babies?"

Smiling slightly, Tucker folded his arms across his chest. "I didn't believe it, Mrs. McCormack, but I have to follow every lead. Obviously the rattle was stolen from the estate. Do you have any idea who took it?"

"Quentin asked me about that." She tapped her lip. "I've been giving the matter some thought. And I do remember a girl who used to work here. She was the upstairs maid. I recall her admiring the heirlooms displayed in one of the bedrooms."

"Do you remember her name?" Tucker asked, instantly alert.

"Josie, I think."

"A last name would be helpful," he said.

Amanda frowned, looking thoughtful. "She was a teenager, a sweet little thing. Her last name began with a D. Give me a minute." She grinned and snapped her fingers. "I've got it. Douglas. Josie Douglas."

Tucker nodded with satisfaction. "I'll check it out."

"Not tonight," Quentin said. "Surely even the law gets a break once in a while."

"He pushes himself really hard," Emma said, looking up at the tall man who had taken her under his wing.

Dana couldn't help wondering if the Queen of Hearts might want to give them a little nudge in the romance department.

"I don't work that hard," Tucker answered. He looked uncomfortable with the attention. "Storkville's normally a quiet little town. Although I'm still investigating Emma's mugging, as well as looking for the mother of the twins. But tomorrow is soon enough to try and get a lead on her."

"Hannah and Jackson treat those children like their own." Dana glanced around the group. "The last time I talked to her, I got the feeling she didn't want to give them up."

Tucker nodded. "They don't lack for attention, that's for sure." He glanced at the auburn-haired woman beside him. "Emma can't seem to stay away from Sammy and Steffie."

She smiled at the mention of the babies. "He's right. I feel as if I need to be near them all the time," she confessed.

"Have you any idea about your past?" Carter asked.

She shook her head. "I've been having memory flashes, but nothing fits together yet."

"I'm sure it's only a matter of time," Dana said. "Maybe if you just relax and try not to force it, your memory will just come back."

"That's what the doctor suggested," she admitted.

"Enough. No more shoptalk." Amanda held out her arms. "Your assignment is to spread out and mingle.

And I'm issuing a royal decree. Everyone is hereby ordered to have a good time,'' she said.

While they'd talked, other people had arrived. Amanda and Carter went off to greet their guests. Tucker and Emma slipped away to carry out his mother's decree. Suddenly Quentin and Dana were alone.

''Your folks were wonderful to the Hewitts,'' Dana said, looking up at him. ''They're with the triplets now, getting reacquainted while they do bedtime duty.''

''I hope they brought raincoats,'' he said wryly.

She laughed. Feeling suddenly awkward, she looked around. From where she stood in the foyer, she could see the great room and part of the front room. ''The house looks wonderful, so festive.''

''If you like ghouls, graveyards and ghosts—oh my!'' Quentin said.

She shook her head at his teasing. With the tip of her finger, she touched the cobwebs on the plant in the center of the circular table. ''I'm not saying I would choose it as a primary decorating motif. But it definitely sets a mood for Halloween.'' She glanced at the archways leading to all the rooms off the foyer. ''Someone sure got carried away with the cobwebs. Or there's an army of spiders on the loose.''

''Dana, there's something I want to say—'' He stopped suddenly. ''Damn.''

''What is it?'' she asked, following his gaze.

''That reporter from the *Sentinel.*''

She spotted Barbara Kyle talking to the guests. ''I have a few choice things to say to her.''

She headed toward the newspaperwoman in the front room. It was empty of furniture, in order to accommodate all the guests.

Dana tapped the woman's shoulder. ''Hello, Barbara. May I have a word with you?''

''Of course, Mrs. McCormack.''

Dana showed her into the foyer where Quentin waited. ''Did you hear that my husband's DNA test cleared him of fathering the abandoned twins?''

''Yes,'' she said, having the decency to look embarrassed.

''I didn't see anything about that in the *Sentinel* this morning.''

''We received the information too late for today's edition,'' she explained. ''The story will appear tomorrow.''

''It had better be a really big headline,'' Dana said. ''If I see it buried on the next to the last page—''

''What my wife means to say,'' Quentin interjected diplomatically, ''is that we'd like to see as many positive stories as you wrote negative ones.''

''Yes, sir.'' Barbara shifted nervously.

''And for the record,'' Dana said, ''why are you here tonight?''

''To cover the party. I'm back on the society beat,'' she said.

''Good.'' Dana nodded her head approvingly. ''Learn to be a responsible journalist. And have a nice time,'' she added.

The woman smiled thinly and walked away.

''You're tough as nails.'' Quentin looked down at her.

''I took a lesson from your mother. That reporter had it coming, and more. If you hadn't stepped in when you did—''

''And a good thing for you, Miss Scarlett. I thought I was going to have to take you to my room for a time-out.''

"Please," she whispered fervently. If being alone with Quentin was punishment, then she wanted to be in trouble for the rest of her life.

"I've been waiting patiently to talk to you, and I can't—"

"Quentin, there you are." Cleland Knox stood just behind them. "I just wanted to say I never believed those rumors about you fathering the twins."

Quentin turned to look at him. "Mr. Mayor, I mean this the nicest possible way—get lost. I want to talk to my wife. No offense."

"None taken, son. Catch you two later," the big man said with a wink and a smile.

Quentin backed her as far into the corner as they could go. "I'd take you outside for some privacy, but it's too damn cold."

"You could keep me warm," she suggested, feigning primness.

He slanted her a roguish look. "Don't tempt me. Now before someone else interrupts, what in the world were you thinking?"

"Which time?" she asked. But she knew what he meant.

"Yesterday. Giving those results to the judge without opening them? Your kids were on the line, lady."

"No, they weren't," she said confidently. "I knew what the results were without looking. There's no way you would turn your back on a child—any child. You're my hero, Quentin. And when the *Sentinel* puts out your good press, McCormack stock will go through the roof."

"You're psychic?"

"No. But the Storkville stork is."

He shook his head as if to clear it. "I'm sorry. I guess I'm a little slow. You want to explain that one?"

"Legend has it that the stork who visits Storkville bestows many bouncing bundles on those whose love is boundless. My bouncing bundles were born in Omaha. But the stork who brought them *knew* I would find my boundless love in Storkville."

Her knees went weak as the corners of his mouth turned up in a lazy half smile. "Any idea who your boundless love is, so I can beat him up?"

She laughed. "How many guys could there be in this town with the initials Q.M.? And he answers to the nickname Mr. Mac." She cleared her throat and met his gaze so that he could see she meant every word. "You are the most wonderful man in the whole world, Quentin McCormack. I love you." She met the intensity in his blue eyes with some of her own. "And if you can forgive me for ever doubting you, this would be the time for flowery romantic declarations."

He took her hands into his own. "I love you too, Dana Hewitt McCormack. From the first moment I saw you."

"I don't believe it. My son had just slimed you."

"It's true. The minute I laid eyes on you, I didn't feel goo, or anything except my heart pounding."

"Considering the magnitude of the slime, I could argue with that, but I'm afraid I *would* win."

He shook his head. "It was love at first sight. But since I didn't believe in it, I couldn't understand why I blurted out a marriage proposal after knowing you such a short time."

"Then I'm a convert too, because it explains why I said yes."

"If I ever meet that psychic stork, I must remember to thank him." He pulled her into the doorway.

"What are you doing?" she asked.

"It's tradition. Haven't you heard? A guy has to kiss

the girl he's standing with under the Halloween cobwebs,'' he said with a grin. ''Then the two are guaranteed a lifetime of happiness.''

''You're starting to make up things like Aunt Gertie,'' she accused.

''Come to think of it, I know where to get some of her top-secret lemonade, awaiting patent approval. If you're game,'' he added.

She knew what he meant. A baby of their own. There was nothing she wanted more. ''I'm game. But my love is so boundless, I'm afraid of how many bouncing bundles the stork would leave if he actually found me in Storkville this time.''

''The more the merrier,'' he said. ''There couldn't be too many for us to handle together.''

He lowered his mouth to hers. The joining of their lips, always warm and wonderful, was even better than before. Because now they each knew that their love was given and received.

Several moments later when he pulled away, Quentin was breathing hard. ''I picked a hell of a time to start this tradition. It would be rude to ignore the guests and take you upstairs for the next installment of the cobweb kiss. I mean sharing a bed.''

''Why, Mistah Butlah,'' she said, her voice breathless, ''are you makin' an unseemly advance?''

''I'm doing my best,'' he said fervently.

''Good.''

''Okay.'' He took her hand and led her toward the right staircase. ''Rhett carried Scarlett up stairs not unlike these.''

''I wouldn't advise it, if you value a healthy back,'' she said ruefully. ''And I seem to recall that they had big problems after that little scene.''

"Come to think of it, later I need to have a word with the Queen of Hearts about her choice of costumes for us."

"Why? Rhett and Scarlett were in love," she said, keeping step as they mounted the stairs.

"But they didn't find their happy ending."

"I read the book." As they reached the landing, she leaned her head against his arm. "And in my own mind I added one more scene. Rhett and Scarlett talked, admitted they'd both made mistakes, and they lived happily ever after."

"Just like us," he said staring down at her with love in his eyes.

"Exactly like us," she answered fervently.

* * * * *

Don't miss

HER HONOR-BOUND LAWMAN

by

Karen Rose Smith,

the final installment of
STORKVILLE, USA, *coming to you*
from Silhouette Romance
in November 2000.

For a sneak preview,
please turn the page

The sound of Tucker's SUV pulling into the driveway had alerted Emma to his return. He'd said he would be late. She'd decided to wait up for him, to spend a few minutes with one of the few people she felt familiar with. The bump on her head had wiped out her past, and she was struggling to deal with that. What if she never remembered? What if she had to just go on from here?

Aunt Gertie, Tucker and the workers at the day-care center where she volunteered were the only people she knew in the world. When Tucker had offered her a room under his roof, she'd been reluctant to accept, but Aunt Gertie—as most of the town called her—had soothed Emma's doubts with something she'd already known deep in her soul. Aunt Gertie had said, "Sheriff Tucker Malone is the most honorable man I know. He'll keep you safe, and he'll do everything in his power to find out who you are."

Hearing the garage door close, Emma took a deep breath. She didn't know what her experience with men in the past had been. Not much, apparently, because after the doctor at the hospital had examined her, he'd told her she was still a virgin. Whatever it had been, she suspected Tucker Malone was the sexiest man she'd ever laid eyes on.

She heard his boots on the linoleum in the kitchen. She heard him walk through the dining room. When he appeared in the doorway to the living room, her heart skipped a beat.

He was at least six-two, with dark brown hair, enhanced by a bit of silver at the temples, that skimmed the collar of his tan sheriff's shirt. His shoulders were broad, and the dark brown stripe that went down the sides of his trousers emphasized his long legs. Her gaze met his. As always, the strength and intensity she found in his dark brown eyes awed her, so much so that her mouth went dry. She'd learned he was a man of few words most of the time. He'd checked on her often when she'd been at Aunt Gertie's. Although she'd been under *his* roof for three days, she still didn't know much about him.

His brows arched up now, and she knew it was an inquiry asking why she was still up.

She motioned to the two glasses she'd set on a tray on the dark pine coffee table and managed to find her voice. "I thought you might like some cider."

Leaning against the doorway, not making a move to come sit beside her on the tan and green plaid sofa, he asked, "Did many kids come to the door for trick-or-treat?"

"I gave out all of the candy and popcorn balls. But I have a few cookies left." She gestured to the dish sitting between the glasses.

Tucker crossed to her slowly, and she saw his gaze

linger on her hair, then pass down the emerald-green sweater and slacks that she wore. Everything inside of her seemed to race, and she felt heat stain her cheeks. She fingered the necklace with "Emma" engraved on it that hung around her neck, the only proof of who she was.

"Did you make these?" he asked gruffly.

She nodded.

When he'd invited her to stay with him, she'd accepted under the terms that she would cook and clean house in exchange for her board.

Tucker picked up one of the cookies and ate it. "I haven't tasted a peanut-butter cookie in years. They're good, Emma."

"Thank you," she murmured, studying his expression, wondering if the faint lines around his eyes had come from happy or sad times. His face was rugged rather than handsome, his jaw strong, his beard shadow evident now, adding to his masculine appeal.

Tucker broke eye contact and took the remote control from her hand. His fingers brushed her palm, and the heat from their touch infused her whole body. When his arm brushed hers as he lowered the volume on the TV, Emma's heart pounded. As she glanced at Tucker, she saw he was gazing at her. Ever since the night she'd been mugged and he'd taken her to the hospital, this...electricity had crackled between them. Whenever she was close to him, she wanted to get closer. The golden sparks in his brown eyes now told her he might want that, too.

"Emma," he said, his voice husky.

She was afraid to move, afraid to answer him, afraid he'd back away. So she just looked up at him, wanting something she couldn't name, wanting to get to know him, wanting the man-woman connection she'd felt with him from the night they'd met.

When he bent his head slowly, she guessed he was waiting for her to lean away. But she wasn't going anywhere. His arm came around her as his lips brushed hers. The brushing became a meeting, the meeting became a hunger, the hunger became a kiss that made bells ring and the earth move. Emma didn't know if she'd ever been kissed before, or what to do next, but her lips parted and Tucker's tongue became masterful and possessive and demanding. She gave herself up to all of it, reveling in his need as well as hers, in something she imagined was desire but seemed like so much more.

Lost in Tucker Malone, Emma was excited by every new sensation...until abruptly he pulled away.

In a terse voice, he said, "That was a mistake, Emma. It won't happen again."

It took her a few moments to realize the magic was gone and Tucker regretted what had happened. Still trembling, she didn't want him to notice. She didn't want him to see how he'd affected her. Because he was right. The kiss *had* been a mistake.

She couldn't get involved with anyone until she remembered who she was....

#1 *New York Times* bestselling author

NORA ROBERTS

introduces the loyal and loving, tempestuous and tantalizing Stanislaski family.

Coming in November 2000:

The Stanislaski Brothers

Mikhail and Alex

Their immigrant roots and warm, supportive home had made Mikhail and Alex Stanislaski both strong and passionate. And their charm makes them irresistible....

And in February 2001, watch for

THE STANISLASKI SISTERS:

Natasha and Rachel

Available at your favorite retail outlet.

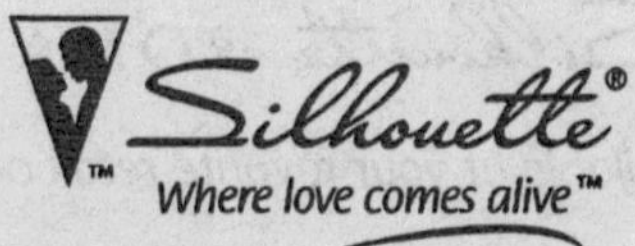

Visit Silhouette at www.eHarlequin.com

PSSTANBR

Desire celebrates Silhouette's 20th anniversary in grand style!

Don't miss:

• ***The Dakota Man* by Joan Hohl**
Another unforgettable MAN OF THE MONTH
On sale October 2000

• ***Marriage Prey* by Annette Broadrick**
Her special anniversary title!
On sale November 2000

• ***Slow Fever* by Cait London**
Part of her new miniseries FREEDOM VALLEY
On sale December 2000

Plus:

FORTUNE'S CHILDREN: THE GROOMS
On sale August through December 2000
Exciting new titles from Leanne Banks, Kathryn Jensen, Shawna Delacorte, Caroline Cross and Peggy Moreland

Every woman wants to be loved…
BODY & SOUL
Desire's highly sensuous new promotion features stories from Jennifer Greene, Anne Marie Winston and Dixie Browning!

Available at your favorite retail outlet.

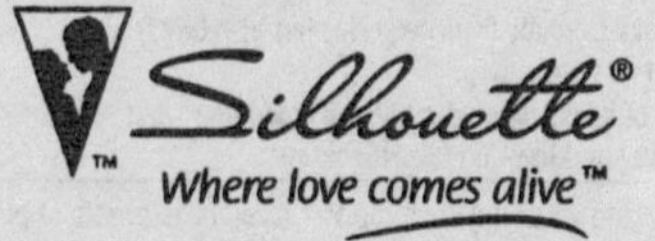

Visit Silhouette at www.eHarlequin.com

PS20SD

COMING NEXT MONTH

#1480 HER HONOR-BOUND LAWMAN—Karen Rose Smith
Storkville, USA
He was tall, dark and older, and he took her in when she'd had no home…or identity. When Emma Douglas's memory returned, she believed she and Sheriff Tucker Malone could have a future. But would the honor-bound lawman she'd come to love accept her in his bed…and in his heart?

#1481 RAFFLING RYAN—Kasey Michaels
The Chandlers Request…
"Sold for $2,000!" With those words wealthy Ryan Chandler reluctantly became earthy Janna Monroe's "date" for a day. Though bachelors for auction seemed ludicrous to Ryan, even crazier was his sudden desire to ditch singlehood for this single mom!

#1482 THE MILLIONAIRE'S WAITRESS WIFE—Carolyn Zane
The Brubaker Brides
For heiress turned waitress Elizabeth Derovencourt, money equaled misery. But her family, not their fortune, mattered. So she visited her ailing grandmother…with a dirt-poor denim-clad cowboy in tow as her "husband." Only she hadn't banked on Dakota Brubaker's irresistible charm—or his millions!

#1483 THE DOCTOR'S MEDICINE WOMAN—Donna Clayton
Single Doctor Dads
Dr. Travis Westcott wanted to adopt twin Native American boys, which was why he welcomed medicine woman Diana Chapman into his home. But somehow the once-burned beauty made Travis want to propose *another* addition to his family: a wife!

#1484 THE THIRD KISS—Leanna Wilson
The first kiss was purely attraction. Brooke Watson and Matt Cutter didn't believe in lasting love. But everyone else did, particularly their nagging families, which was why Brooke agreed to playact the tycoon's beaming bride-to-be. Yet as a *real* wedding date loomed, was a happily-ever-after possible?

#1485 THE WEDDING LULLABY—Melissa McClone
Their marriage had lasted only one night. No problems, no heartache. But unexpectedly Laurel Worthington found herself expecting! When she told father-to-be Brett Matthews her news, he insisted they marry again. But Laurel wasn't about to settle for anything but the *real* golden ring....